Blanche clapped her erasers a few more times. Then she said, "You haven't been in school here before. How did you learn so many spelling words?"

"My mama taught me," said Rose. She did not like the tone of Blanche's voice, but she tried to be polite anyway. "She was a schoolteacher once. I like to read, too. I learned many words from reading books."

"Well, anyone can see that plain as day," Blanche said tartly. "It's all you do, read and stare out the window and be teacher's pet. But don't think we can be friends just because you are so smart. After all, you're a country girl."

With that, Blanche flounced off to return her erasers. Rose's face stung as though it had been slapped. Alva was right, Rose thought angrily. Town girls are stuck up.

Rose decided then and there that she would never, ever let Blanche Coday spell her down.

BE SURE TO READ OTHER BOOKS IN

THE LITTLE HOUSE FAMILY

LITTLE TOWN ON THE PRAIRIE

THESE HAPPY GOLDEN YEARS

THE FIRST FOUR YEARS

By Cynthia Rylant:

OLD TOWN IN THE GREEN GROVES

Laura Ingalls Wilder's

Lost Little House Years

The Rose Years

Laura's daughter, born 1886

LITTLE HOUSE ON ROCKY RIDGE

LITTLE FARM IN THE OZARKS

ADDITIONAL LITTLE HOUSE BOOKS

NELLIE OLESON MEETS LAURA INGALLS

LITTLE FARM
IN THE OZARKS

by ROGER LEA MacBRIDE

HarperTrophy®
An Imprint of HarperCollins*Publishers*

HarperTrophy®, ☎®, Little House®, and The Rose Years™
are trademarks of HarperCollins Publishers.

Library of Congress Cataloging-in-Publication Data
MacBride, Roger Lea.
    Little Farm in the Ozarks / Roger Lea MacBride — Abridged
HarperTrophy ed.
        p. cm.
    Summary: An abridged version of the story of Laura and Almanzo Wilder
and their eight-year-old daughter Rose as they continue to work making
Rocky Ridge farm in Missouri their new home.
    ISBN 978-0-06-114810-1
    1. Wilder, Laura Ingalls, 1867–1957—Juvenile fiction. [1. Wilder, Laura
Ingalls, 1867–1957—Fiction. 2. Frontier and pioneer life—Missouri—
Fiction. 3. Missouri—Fiction.] I. Title.
PZ7.M12255Lf 2007   2007011854
[Fic]—dc22   CIP
                                                              AC

Typography by Christopher Stengel
❖
First Harper Trophy Edition, 1994
Abridged Harper Trophy Edition, 2007

For my daughter Abby,
Who shares with me the legacy of Rose.
In them both, God got it right.

CONTENTS

CONTENTS

THIEF!

Rose was sitting at the table in the little log house on Rocky Ridge Farm, finishing a letter to Grandma Ingalls, when she heard snarling coming from outside. Fido raised his head from the hearth and growled deep in his chest.

"What was that?" Rose asked.

Mama closed her book and looked at Papa.

"Might be it's just a bobcat," he said, "but I'd best check the horses." He set down the leather horse collar he was oiling and wiped his hands on a rag.

Papa lit the lantern and pulled on his heavy buffalo coat before taking his gun down from its rack. "Stay here, boy," he told Fido, who had followed him to the door. "I can handle this." A cold gust of wind blew in when Papa opened the door.

Rose read her letter to herself:

"Dear Grandma," she had written. "Thank you very much for the good, warm socks, and for sending us the *De Smet News* every week. I am reading the story about poor General Custer.

"It is not so cold here as South Dakota, but my feet get cold sometimes. It snowed today. But Papa said spring will come soon, even if it is just February! I like Missouri, but I miss everyone so very much. Your loving grand-daughter, Rose."

Rose and her mother both looked up when Papa came back inside.

"Everything seems to be in order," he said. "The horses are quiet, and I don't see any strange tracks in the snow."

Papa went back to oiling the collar. "I was thinking, Bess," he said to Mama. "I'll be needing some help around the place come spring. Reynolds at the general store told me that, here in the Ozarks, folks plant their peas in February and their potatoes in March."

"I can scarcely believe it, Manly," Mama said. "We never planted anything before April in South Dakota. Are you sure he wasn't pulling the wool over your eyes?"

"I wouldn't have believed it myself," Papa said. "But Reynolds has his onion sets and seed potatoes in stock already."

Suddenly Fido barked. They all heard a burst of cackling.

"The henhouse!" Mama cried out. Rose's heart fluttered in her chest.

Papa and Mama jumped up at the same time. Papa grabbed his gun again, and they both rushed out the door with Fido leading the way.

Rose shivered in the doorway as she watched the lantern light disappear into the henhouse.

Finally Mama and Papa came walking back. When they drew close, Rose was shocked to see a boy with them! Papa gripped him by the arm. The boy jerked his shoulder, trying to pull away. Rose backed into the house and they all came in.

"All right, son," Papa said in his most sober voice. "Now just you calm down a spell. Have a seat over there, by the table."

The boy sat down with a huff. His thin, pale face poked out of clothing that looked like a pile of old rags. He wore a man's threadbare suit jacket that hung to his knees and his pants were man's pants that had been cut off and patched. They were so big the pockets hung on the inside of his legs. His patched shirt was made of flour sacks, and the soles of his shoes flapped loose.

"Now, son," Papa said. "Let's have your name."

The boy stared at the floor in silence.

"Stealing is serious business," Papa told him. "We can go into town and talk to the sheriff, if you like. Now why don't you tell us, who are your folks?"

"Ain't got none," the boy muttered in a raspy voice. He shivered and hugged himself.

Rose couldn't take her eyes off him. The boy

looked about her age, which was eight, or perhaps a bit older. His ears stood out, and his nose was too big. His blue eyes seemed to show nothing at all.

"Everybody has folks somewhere," Papa said. "Are you from these parts?"

"I ain't from nowhere," the boy said defiantly. Rose thought she saw his mouth wobble in the flickering firelight. Mama and Papa looked at each other over the boy's head.

Papa's eyes shone with a gentle warmth. "If you're hungry we might be able to scare up a bite or two."

The boy looked at Papa for the first time.

"Are you hungry, son?"

The boy nodded. Papa let him sit warming in front of the fire while Mama put up some beans and cold potatoes in the spider-legged skillet to heat in the fireplace. Rose spotted a tear glittering on the boy's cheek.

"I'm Mr. Wilder," Papa said. "This is my wife, and our daughter, Rose."

"Hello," Rose said softly. The boy looked at her, but his face was blank. She could not tell what he was thinking.

"I'm Swiney," the boy finally said. "Swiney Baird. It's just me and my big brother, Abe."

"What about your folks, your ma and pa?"

"Dead," Swiney said simply.

His eyes followed Mama lifting the skillet out of the fireplace and spooning the steaming beans and potatoes onto a plate.

"All right, Swiney," Mama said. "Come and eat."

Swiney pulled his chair over to the table and spooned the hot food into his mouth as fast as he could. Rose had never seen anyone eat so fast.

When he was finished, Mama took the empty plate away. Swiney stood up and looked around the little log house, as if to leave. But Papa motioned with his hand to sit back down.

"Now, then," Papa said. "Let's see if I have this right. Your folks have passed on, and you live with your brother. Where is that?"

Swiney pursed his mouth and stared into his lap. "Yonder," he said after a long pause, jerking his thumb. "On Kinnebrew's place. In the tenant house."

"Kinnebrew," Mama said slowly. "Aren't they the folks who moved here from Illinois last fall?"

Swiney nodded his head.

"Well, surely they would take you in for a meal."

Swiney shook his head gravely. "They don't like us country jakes." Then he looked at Mama, his eyes suddenly wide with fear. "You ain't a-going to tell them, is you? There wasn't no real harm in it, honest. I was just a-looking for eggs is all."

"Don't you worry about that," Papa said. "The important thing is that you don't have to steal from us to eat, Swiney. We'd never let a boy go hungry if we had a crumb to spare. Where is your brother now?"

Swiney wiped his nose with the back of his dirty hand. His nails were chipped. "He drove a load of timber to Cabool."

"Cabool is a good two days' wagon trip," said Papa. "You must stay here with us tonight."

"But I cain't," Swiney whined, standing up. "I got to be going, mister."

"You'll stay here, son, and that's final," Papa said.

Swiney's shoulders slumped and he looked as if he was about to cry. But he sat quietly as Mama got out extra quilts and made up his bed.

When they were all settled for the night, Rose couldn't sleep. She did not think she liked Swiney very much. He was a thief, he was dirty, and he hadn't thanked Mama for his supper. But she was sorry he had no mother or father.

And it *was* something new to have a stranger in the house. So far, their first winter in Missouri had been lonely. Rose had to stay home from school until Mama and Papa could get a little money ahead. Mama had said Rose could start school in July, when the next session began. Until then, Mama was teaching Rose her studies.

It had been too cold to explore outdoors or play with her friend Alva, who lived nearby. Her only other friends were Paul and George Cooley, who had come with Rose's family to Missouri from South Dakota. When they weren't in school, Paul and George helped their mama and papa run the Mansfield Hotel in town. Rose saw Paul and George only on Sunday, when the two families went to church.

Rose's restless thoughts were interrupted by Swiney crying out in his sleep, "Mumphster fluff!" Rose was curious about him. She wondered about his life, and how he got such a funny name.

NEW FRIENDS

When Rose woke up in the chilly dawn, Swiney was gone. He had slipped out of the house before the first rooster crow.

"Why did he leave?" asked Rose.

"I expect he was afraid we would change our minds and turn him over to the sheriff," said Papa. "That little shaver's as bold as a sparrow. I'm sure last night wasn't the first time he found himself in a fix."

The day dawned warm and soft. Before dinnertime, the snow had turned mushy. While Rose helped Mama with the wash, she noticed a strange noise coming from the direction of Fry Creek. It sounded like a multitude of tiny bells, or many people whistling.

"I hear it, too," said Mama. "I wonder what it could be? It's too early for grasshoppers and crickets."

After dinner, Rose walked down toward the creek to explore. The whistling sound seemed to be coming from a marshy place near the water's edge. Rose stepped on a fallen branch, which crackled under her foot. Immediately she saw several splashes in the water, and the noise stopped. She squatted at the edge of the swamp and looked closely into it.

There were some bubbles close together that seemed to move. Rose stared at those bubbles for the longest time, until finally she saw that they were a tiny pair of frog's eyes and a little frog's nose floating in the murky water. But as long as she sat there, no frogs would peep.

She walked a little way from the swampy area and listened. It lightened her soul to hear those frogs singing their hearts out once again. Rose realized with astonishment that even though it was still winter, this was the very first sound of spring.

Rose was telling Mama about the peeping frogs when Papa came riding home on May. Behind him, riding together on a mule with notched ears, were a young man and Swiney.

The man and Swiney dismounted and stood before Mama and Rose. Swiney stared at the ground and kicked at a clump of snow.

"This is my wife and our daughter, Rose," Papa said. "Bess, Rose, this is Abe Baird, Swiney's big brother."

"Hello," Rose said politely.

"Pleased to make your acquaintance," Abe said in a warm, deep voice. His face was young and smooth, like a boy's. But it was also strong and bony, like a grown man's. A great shock of black hair fell across his forehead. Rose couldn't help staring at him. He didn't look anything like Swiney at all.

"It's like I was a-telling Mr. Wilder, ma'am," he said to Mama. "Swiney's and me's ma died birthing our baby sister. I reckon she was wore out after a-bringing twelve little ones into this world. The apoplexy carried off

Pa just six months after."

"Twelve children," Mama said in wonderment. "However did you manage? Where are the rest?"

"We stuck together for a spell," Abe said. "But we durn near starved. In time, the little ones was a-taken in here and there. The older ones went out to find work. Swiney here always was a fractious little hornet, so I kept him on with me.

"But I ain't been much of a pa. I'm real sorry about last night. I told Swiney, stealing ain't no path to go. I brung you some meat in this here poke, to show no harm meant." He reached into a sack at his feet and pulled out a dead raccoon by the tail."

"Well, thank you, but I don't think . . ." Mama began. "I mean, I wouldn't know the first thing about cooking a . . . what is it?"

"Coon, ma'am," said Abe. "It's some of the best eating meat we got in these here hills. Swiney and I'll skin it, and I can tell you just how to cook it."

Mama looked at Papa. The color drained

from her face. But there was nothing more she could politely say. Abe would not take no for an answer, and Mama would never argue against the generosity of strangers. So, Abe and Swiney stayed to supper of roast raccoon and turnips. After they had ridden away on their mule, Papa announced that Abe was going to be their hired hand.

"Are you sure he's reliable?" asked Mama. "Isn't he sharecropping for Mr. Kinnebrew?"

"He is," Papa said. "But he's also cutting railroad ties and fence rails on his own. He's a good strong boy, just a little young and rough around the edges is all. And Swiney can help with the chores around the place."

"Very well," Mama said. "You can never tell through what door Providence may walk."

After breakfast the next morning, Abe and Swiney came back.

"You listen to Mrs. Wilder same as if she was our ma," Abe told Swiney before going off with Papa to the woodlot.

"Now, Swiney," Mama said. "First thing we need to do is get you a good, hot bath."

"A bath?" Swiney said in a whining voice. "But why? Abe don't make me take no bath."

"I'm not Abe," Mama said, "and you've got skunk scent in all your clothes."

Swiney took his bath in a corner of the house behind a sheet Mama had hung from the rafters. While he splashed around in the tin tub, Mama scrubbed his threadbare clothes with soft soap in the big cast-iron pot outside. She gave him Rose's extra flannel union suit to wear while he sat in a chair and waited for his things to dry.

When he was dressed again, Mama said Rose could show him around the farm.

Rose kept her thoughts to herself as they walked by the henhouse. Swiney stared at the ground until they had passed it.

Then Rose showed Swiney the new barn that their neighbors had helped Papa build one day in the fall. They looked at the mares, Pet and May, in their stalls and fed handfuls of oats to the colts, Little Pet and Prince. Soon they would be old enough to sell. Rose hated to think of it, but she knew they couldn't keep the colts forever.

They walked toward the apple orchard. Swiney pulled out a folding knife and began to sharpen it by scraping it on a whetstone he carried in his pocket. He spit on his arm and shaved off a tiny patch of the fine, damp hair.

"Why did you do that?" Rose asked.

"To see if it's right sharp," Swiney said. "That's how to tell."

"Can I try it?"

"Girls ain't supposed to play with knives," Swiney scoffed. "Besides, this here was my pa's knife. Abe gave it to me and I ain't never let nobody else touch it." He wiped the blade on his pants, snapped it shut, and dropped it back in his pocket.

Fido sniffed for rabbits around the brush piles left from Papa's clearing the land. As soon as the ground had thawed enough, Papa would replant all of the slender young apple saplings that had come with Rocky Ridge Farm when they first moved there in the fall.

"When I am thirteen years old, all those trees will bear apples," Rose explained.

Mama and Papa had brought Rose here

from South Dakota to get away from a drought. They had packed all their belongings into a little black wagon and driven to Missouri, The Land of the Big Red Apple. They bought the little run-down farm, called it Rocky Ridge, and began to fix it up. The farm came with nearly a thousand apple saplings all heeled in, waiting to be planted. In a few years, those apple trees would begin to bear fruit that Mama and Papa could sell. They would never want for anything again.

But for now, Rose knew they must make do with what they had.

Rose and Swiney were walking through the woods around the apple orchard when Swiney suddenly stopped and peered up at a particular tree.

"Want to play tree-topping?" he asked.

"What is that?"

"You ain't never tree-topped?" Swiney said, his eyes wide with amazement. "Just you watch."

Swiney climbed up the tree as quick as a squirrel. When he got near the top, it began to bend under his weight. He grabbed hold of a thin branch over his head. He let his legs swing out. Slowly, with a little groan, the tree bent until Swiney's feet touched the ground.

Then he began to jump up and down, still holding the top of the little tree. Each time he came back down he bounced a little higher. Finally he bounced so high that the tree stood straight up and then bent all the way down on the other side until his feet touched the ground. Swiney had ridden that tree all the way over the top!

Rose had never seen anything like it. "Let me try!" she shouted.

Swiney stopped bouncing, but he held on to the branch. "Come and grab on," he said. Rose took it and held on as tight as she could. She felt the springiness in it.

"Now start a-jumping is all," Swiney said. "Don't let go."

Rose took a little jump, but her feet barely left the ground.

"Come on," Swiney said. "Jump high, and keep a-jumping, high as you can."

Rose jumped higher and higher. She felt

herself starting to fly. She laughed.

Finally she pushed off with all her might. She felt herself going up and up into the sky, as if she would never come down. Then she heard a loud crack, like a gunshot. The branch she was holding didn't feel springy anymore.

Now she really *was* flying, spinning sickeningly, away from the tree. Then she was falling and falling, for the longest time.

In an instant, everything came to a stop with a horrible *thud* that stole her breath. Lights exploded in her head.

Rose tried to get up, but she could not move. She was in a peculiar, misty place of no sound, no time, and no color. There was only a warm stinging in her face, and the ringing in her ears, like bumblebees trapped in a jug.

Faintly, through the buzzing, Rose heard Swiney calling her name.

"Wha-what happened?" Rose asked in a quavering voice.

"That old treetop broke right off," said Swiney. "You sure went a-flying."

Rose slowly got up, brushing off her coat.

Her legs wobbled at first, but then she felt like herself again and laughed.

"That was fun," she said. "I want to do it again. I mean, without it breaking."

Swiney picked another tree. He bent it extra hard to be sure it wouldn't break. Then they took turns tree-topping. Rose thought nothing else could ever be so much fun.

"What on earth have you been up to?" Mama exclaimed when they got back to the house. "Your face is scratched, your braids are all undone, and your coat! It's torn."

"I was running. And . . . and I fell," Rose fibbed. She didn't want to tell Mama about tree-topping. She stole a sideways glance at Swiney. He was grinning at her. Rose struggled to keep her face straight.

"You were just running and fell?" Mama asked. She raised an eyebrow doubtfully as she looked at Swiney and then back at Rose.

Rose held her breath. She was just about to tell Mama the truth when Mama sighed. "All right, then," she said. "Come sit while I dab some coal oil on those scratches. Then you two wildcats can gather some firewood. Abe and Swiney are staying to supper."

Rose still did not know if she liked Swiney. He was rough, and she could not forget that he had tried to steal from her family. But they had had fun playing together.

Later that night, Rose had a special feeling. It was a feeling like the peeping of frogs and the lengthening of days, of newness and change. The rustle of spring was everywhere.

Fresh Greens

Gentle spring rains fell all the next week, slowly melting the remaining snow and softening the earth.

When Abe and Swiney had stayed to help Mr. Kinnebrew one day, Papa hitched the mares to the plow. He began to work the new ground he had cleared for the garden, the orchard, and the crops. But almost as soon as he started, Papa came back to the house with a frown on his face and covered in mud.

"It's as if the bottom dropped out of the earth!" he said. "Nothing but mud. The worst of it is, the horses' hooves sink right into it.

They hurt themselves trying to pull out."

"Surely you can wait a bit, until the ground dries some," Mama said.

"I can but I shouldn't," said Papa. "There's too much work to be done. We'll have to trade the colts for a pair of mules. They have narrow feet that won't hurt the garden or get stuck in the mud."

"It was bound to come to this sooner or later," said Mama. "We had to borrow Mr. Stubbins's mules last fall to plow the ground for the garden. The colts are broken now, and there's no sense wearing out the poor mares."

So Papa put leads on Little Pet and Prince and walked them away from Rocky Ridge Farm. Rose could not stifle a sob as she watched them go. She remembered how the little colts had trotted alongside their mothers on the hard, dusty trip from South Dakota. She remembered how Prince would nuzzle her arm asking for a carrot and the time Papa had let her sit on Little Pet as he led the colt around the barn. Now she would never ride Little Pet again.

"You mustn't cry," said Mama, hugging

Rose to her. "There is no work for the colts here, anyway. They will be happier pulling a buggy in town and getting some exercise."

When Papa came back with the mules, Rose did not go to look at them. They were not beautiful and graceful like horses; they were bred for work, not for riding.

The next day Papa hitched up the mules and plowed the garden. The mules had to fight every inch of the way through the roots and rocks. The soil was as sticky as pudding. Everywhere Rose walked there was reddish-brown mud.

After Papa finished plowing the garden, Mama and Rose went to work hoeing it smooth. Pools of water stood in the holes where Papa had taken out stumps. For days and days, they picked stones out of the mud, and Swiney came to help.

"Where did all these stones come from?" Rose asked with a weary sigh. They had picked stones out of the garden in the fall until the soil was clean. But now it was full of them again.

"I don't know," said Mama, pushing her

hair from her face. Her cheek was streaked with mud. "The earth here is very thin. It just seems to grow them."

Slowly, it grew warmer. Shyly at first, then more boldly, the forest birds rehearsed their spring voices. "Cheerio! Cheerio! Cheerio!" the robins sang. Brilliant red cardinals cried, "What cheer! What cheer! What cheer!" Little white-throated sparrows called out, "Old Tom Peabody, Peabody, Peabody."

Rose whistled those songs as she worked. All the woods seemed to be a bustle of mysterious affairs.

Rose was resting from picking up rocks and throwing them to the side of the garden when she saw someone coming through the trees. It was a little girl with fiery red hair sticking out from under her bonnet.

"Alva!" Rose cried out. She had not seen Alva since before Christmas.

"Hello, Rose," Alva said. "Hello, Mrs. Wilder."

"Hello, Alva," Mama said. "What a pleasant surprise. What brings you visiting?"

"Can Rose come and play a spell?" Alva asked. "I found some pokeweed down by Wolf Creek. We could pick you a mess for salad."

"Pokeweed?" said Mama.

"It's greens," Swiney piped up. "And cow parsley. We always eat greens in spring."

"This is Swiney Baird," Rose said. "His big brother, Abe, is my papa's new hired man."

Alva looked at Swiney, but she did not say anything.

"Yes, Rose may go play," said Mama. "Are you sure you know what's good to eat, and what isn't?"

"Yes, ma'am," Alva said. "I help my ma with the picking every year. We ain't never got sick yet."

Rose took a pail from the house and walked down to Wolf Creek with Alva. Swiney trailed behind. Rose told Alva about all the happenings at Rocky Ridge Farm since they had last seen each other.

At Wolf Creek, Alva showed Rose a clump of pokeweed. "You take the little soft leaves, but not the root," Alva explained.

"I got a knife, so I'll be the cutter," Swiney announced. He took out his knife and started sharpening it.

"Who says?" said Alva. "We don't need no cutter, anyway. We can just tear them off."

"Can not!" Swiney shouted.

"Can, too!" Alva shouted back. "You can just go find your own poke and cut it if you like. We don't care."

"Humph!" Swiney grumbled, shaving a little patch of arm hair.

Alva showed Rose how to check to make sure there weren't any bugs or insect eggs hiding on the undersides of the bright green leaves. They tore off the tenderest leaves and dropped them in the pail. On the edge of the creek, growing right out of the clear cold water, they found watercress. "Try it," said Alva. "It's real good."

Rose pulled some of the tiny leaves from the stem and put them in her mouth. Nothing had ever tasted so fresh and tangy, like radishes. Rose had not realized how hungry she was for fresh vegetables.

Alva and Rose were busy picking when

Swiney called out to them: "Watch me! Look! Bet you can't do this!" He was standing on top of a fence. He began to walk shakily along the top rail, holding out his arms for balance.

"That's nothing. We don't care, anyway." Alva sniffed. Just as Swiney got to the end of the section, he tried to turn around. But he lost his balance and fell, head first. Just in the instant before Swiney's head would have hit the ground, one of his pant legs got tangled in the fence. He stopped short, hanging upside down, just above the ground.

"Ow!" he screamed. "I'm stuck!" He twisted and turned, and huffed and kicked. But try as he might, he couldn't unstick himself.

"Ha, ha, ha!" Alva shouted gleefully. "Now I know why they call you Swiney. You got your snout into everything."

Rose giggled. She hadn't thought of it before, but Swiney really did get into things like a rooting hog.

"Get me down," Swiney pleaded. "Help me!"

"Maybe we ought to just leave him there," Alva said, putting her hands on her hips. "It would serve him right, sticking his swiney snout into everything. Whiney Swiney!" she shouted in singsong.

"No," Rose said. She didn't like Swiney as well as she liked Alva, and she could laugh at how foolish he looked. But Rose could never be truly mean, and especially not to Swiney, who had no mother or father.

"Come and help," she said to Alva. Together they lifted up Swiney until his pant leg came loose. Then he fell to the ground in a heap, like a pile of old clothes. When he got up, his face was crimson, and pinched with anger.

"Are you all right?" asked Rose.

"Awww, never mind!" Swiney shouted. He stomped off toward the house.

When the bucket was full of greens, Alva went home. Rose brought the bucket to Mama and helped her wash and parboil the greens in a pot. Then Mama drained off the water and added the greens to the salt pork that was frying in the skillet.

When everything was cooked, they sat down to eat it with chunks of fresh corn bread to sop up the delicious pot liquor. The greens were a little bitter but still refreshing for tongues tired of beans, salt pork, and corn bread.

"That was delicious," Papa said, wiping his mustache with his napkin. "Sure whets a fellow's appetite for real garden food. I'd say it's about time to start planting."

"Yes, the garden is about ready, and it's coming up on a full moon," said Mama. "After that will be time to put in the ground crops. Rose and I will go with you tomorrow to town to pick up seeds and some other provisions."

Rose had hardly been to town since they first moved to Mansfield, only to church on Sunday when everything and everyone were quiet and sober. She had never gone to town with Papa on his errands. Now she looked forward to seeing the town on a market day, full of life. It would be fun to see something different for a change.

Market Day

The next morning, patches of thin mist floated above Wolf Creek as they splashed across the ford to the other side. Then the wagon rumbled alongside it, through the little valley that lay between Rocky Ridge Farm and Mansfield.

"Do you think Reynolds will give us credit enough to get all our spring provisions?" Mama asked over Rose's head.

"Can't see why not," said Papa. "Folks know me now, from my winter job delivering coal oil for Mr. Waters. And I've sold our stove wood to half the houses in town. Anyone can see we're honest, hardworking farmers."

"It just makes me uneasy, Manly," said Mama. "It was hard enough on the prairie, praying all summer for the wheat harvest to come in only to see it blown away by cyclone, or burned up by drought. Now, with taxes and the mortgage and this land so thin and stony, it's a wonder we can raise enough just to—"

"Now, Bess, you're putting the oak before the acorn," Papa interrupted. "Besides, you forget all that timber we have to be made into fence rails and railroad ties. It's cash money we can always count on.

"And the hens will be laying again soon. We've always made out somehow. We always will." He smiled and reached over to squeeze Mama's hand.

Mama sighed and looked out across an orchard of grown apple trees they were passing. Rose prayed that their orchard would hurry and grow.

When the wagon crested a steep hill, Rose could see Mansfield spread out before them. The horses began to trot toward the center of town. Papa had to rein them in to keep their hooves from kicking up clods of mud.

The town square was crowded. Papa had to drive around it twice to find an empty hitching spot.

Some men waved and called out to Papa, "Howdy, Wilder!"

While Papa hitched the team, Mama and Rose brushed off their feet and put on their stockings and shoes. Then they all walked on the gravel path around the square. Mama put her hand through Papa's arm, and held up her skirt from the muddy ground with the other. Rose thought Mama and Papa looked lovely together, walking like that.

In the middle of the square was a park, with trees and a bandstand. The railroad tracks made one side of the square, with the depot for the Kansas City, Fort Scott, and Memphis Railroad. Around the square were the stores that all those people had come to trade in. The signs read, NEWTON'S GROCERIES, CODAY'S DRUGS, THE BANK OF MANSFIELD, OPERA HOUSE, and THE MANSFIELD HOTEL, where Paul and George lived.

"Mama, can we visit the Cooleys? Please?" Rose pleaded.

"No," said Mama. "A hotel is a business. It is not a place for visiting."

Now they came to Reynolds's Store. As they passed from the bright sunlight to the darkness inside, Rose's eyes could see only shadowy shapes.

"Wait here, Rose," said Mama. Then she and Papa walked all the way to the back of the store to speak with Mr. Reynolds.

Slowly Rose's eyes began to see. The store was a wonderland. Everywhere she turned were tables, shelves, rolls, bins, barrels, kegs, and boxes of every imaginable made thing in the world, all piled up every which way.

On the floor around her were sacks of flour and corn meal, bags of potatoes, barrels brimming with pickles, and crackers, and raisins, and kegs of horseshoes and nails. On top of the dark wooden counters, there were piles of men's clothing, coffeepots, dishes, pitchers, and washbasins. There were boxes of seed packets painted with beautiful pictures of shiny red tomatoes, and dark green watermelons, and pale green cabbages.

The shelves on the walls drooped with great bolts of colored fabrics and shiny ribbons. There were boxes of different-colored sewing thread arranged like a rainbow and piles of pencil tablets, schoolbooks, and slates. Even the ceiling had been used to hang water buckets, and tools, and horse collars.

Rose walked farther back into the store, staring as she passed jars and kegs crammed with brightly colored candy. She could smell the peppermint, and it made her mouth water.

"Hello there, young lady," a man's voice boomed out close by. "What can we do for you today?"

A man with a big belly looked down at her. He grinned at her from under a bushy mustache.

"Which one do you like?" he asked.

Rose's ears warmed. She didn't know what to say.

"It's all right," the man said. "I'm Mr. Reynolds. This is my store. Your ma and pa are right over there, giving their order. How about these lemon drops? Do you like them?"

Rose nodded. She had never eaten a lemon drop, but she just knew she would like them. Her heart fluttered as he poured the candy into a little brown bag and handed it to her. She almost forgot to say, "Thank you, Mr. Reynolds."

"You bet," Mr. Reynolds said. He called out to a customer and walked away.

Rose wanted to eat a lemon drop right then, but she would wait to share with Mama and Papa on the ride home.

Mama was holding up a piece of cloth, brown calico with white polka dots. She was going to sew a new school dress for Rose.

"How do you like this, Rose?" Rose looked at the fabric. Then she looked at the other bolts of cloth on the shelves. She had always worn calico and thought she would like gingham for a change. She looked at the blue and red, the blue and black, and at a dark blue and deep lavender.

"That one," Rose said, pointing to the blue and lavender. Rose felt a wave of happiness. She had not had a new dress in almost a year.

She wanted blue hair ribbons to go with her dress, but she knew not to ask. She could have new hair ribbons when Mama said so.

Finally they were finished. Papa backed the wagon up to the sidewalk and loaded everything in. Rose's mouth watered when she saw the big bag of flour. They would have light bread again after a long winter of eating corn bread.

On the short ride home, they ate some of the puckery-sweet lemon drops. The sky was clear and blue. A lone white cloud rose from the horizon in front of them.

In the wagon behind them were new shuck collars for the mules, seeds for the garden, coal oil, sacks of sugar and flour, salt, tea, a big piece of salt pork, molasses, and cloth for new clothes.

"You see, Bess," Papa said. "Reynolds treated us square. We'll have everything we need to get through till settling-up time in the fall, and then some."

FIGHTING MULES

Now began the hard work of planting the garden. First Papa got out the harrow he had made during the winter. He sharpened the wooden teeth with his knife.

Then he hitched the harrow to the mules and they dragged it back and forth until the garden was smooth and soft. Then he hitched the mules to the plow and plowed deep rows in the garden, leaving high ridges of dirt on either side.

Rose helped Mama cut the potatoes into small pieces, making sure each piece had at least two eyes. Then they buried the pieces in the ridges of dirt. They made sure the eyes were facing up so that they could sprout properly.

Then they planted the onion sets and the turnip seeds. Mama planted the tomato seeds in the wooden hotbeds Papa had made. On warm days, she brought the hotbeds out of the house and set them in a sunny place.

One beautiful, warm Sunday after church, Mama said Rose must be good and watch the farm. She and Papa were going back into town to see the Cooleys.

"Can't I go, too?" Rose pleaded. She wanted to play with Paul and George.

"No," said Mama. "Paul and George are staying behind, also, to watch the hotel. We are going for a buggy drive, just Mr. and Mrs. Cooley, Papa, and I."

Rose pouted while Mama changed her dress and then put extra wood in the little stove in the lean-to kitchen. Then Mama put in two loaves of bread to bake. They would be ready when she and Papa came home.

Papa saddled the mares, and Mama and Papa rode off toward town.

"Be good, Rose," Mama called out. "Don't wander off, and watch the stove."

The first thing Rose did was take off her stockings and shoes. At least if she had to stay home alone, she could go barefoot. Her feet were pale from being cooped up all winter. She wiggled her toes. They were happy to be free again.

Then she went outside and sat on a stump in the yard. She listened to the wind sighing in the trees. The first tiny leaves were sprouting, tender and blushing pale pink and yellow and green.

Little white butterflies fluttered here and there, and bumblebees butted and buzzed, starting their nests. Goldfinches and robins fluttered from tree to tree, calling out their spring cheer.

Rose was bored, so she decided to look at the mules. Papa had told her to stay away from them. But Rose thought she would just give them a little salt. The mules loved salt almost as much as they liked the grass. Rose got a handful of salt from the house.

The bay-colored mule was named Roy, for Papa's big brother Royal. Mama had named the gray mule Nellie, after a little girl she had known a long time ago.

When Rose walked into the hallway of the barn, the mules did not come to the stall gates to see her. They stood at the backs of their stalls, eyeing her suspiciously. Rose climbed up on the log wall and laid the salt on top of the low wall that separated their two stalls.

Nellie got to the salt first, and when Roy tried to lick some, Nellie squealed horribly, wheeled around, and kicked at the log walls with all her might. Roy backed up, his ears laid back, snapping at the air with big yellow teeth. Then Nellie wheeled around and started licking again.

The sound of their fighting and braying and squealing was horrible, but it struck Rose as funny, and she shrieked with laughter.

The mules fought, each getting a little lick of salt now and again, until the salt was gone. Rose had been terribly naughty. She blushed just to think of what Mama would say if she knew. But of course she wouldn't.

Rose was trying to think of something else

to do when Swiney came riding up on Abe's mule, Old Guts.

"Howdy, Rose," Swiney called out, sliding off Old Guts's saddle. "What are you doing?"

"Nothing," said Rose. "Mama and Papa went riding. I was playing with the mules. They were fighting over salt. Do you want to see?"

"You bet," he said.

Rose got another handful of salt. This time the mules smelled the salt and started fighting before she even put it down for them. Swiney and Rose laughed and laughed.

Finally they tired of the mules. "Mules are mean," Rose said. "I like horses better. Does Old Guts fight?"

"Naw. He's tame as a kitty-cat. Want to ride him?"

"Could I?" Rose asked eagerly.

Swiney nodded and Rose scrambled up on top of Old Guts and settled into the saddle. Papa had let Rose sit on the mares a few times and had led her around with the halter on Little Pet. But she had never ridden by herself.

"Go on," Swiney said. "Give him a kick."

Rose kicked her heels a little against the mule's sides.

"Aw, come on," Swiney said. "Kick him good."

Rose kicked harder, but Old Guts ignored her and nibbled some grass.

Swiney picked up a stick and swatted Old Guts on the backside with a *whap!*

The mule leaped into the air, tossing his head. Rose pitched forward and her forehead hit him hard between the ears with a *clunk*. Old Guts galloped a few steps, and then stopped short. Rose's head spun. She climbed down trembling from the mule's back. She wobbled a few steps and then sat down hard.

Swiney came running. "What happened?" he shouted.

"I hit my head," Rose groaned. Everything was spinning.

"Uh-oh," Swiney said. "You look like a ghost, Rose. I'll fetch some water."

Swiney brought the wooden water bucket and Rose drank a dipperful. The spinning slowed down, and then she just felt a little woozy.

Rose stood up on wobbly legs. Swiney picked up the water bucket and followed her to the house. Just as she got to the lean-to door, Rose smelled smoke. She remembered Mama's bread cooking in the stove. Out of the corner of her eye, something made her look up.

She glanced at the chimney pipe and gasped. The roof was burning! The house was on fire!

Rose stood there in frozen terror, staring at the orange flames that danced in the breeze. They were growing bigger even while she watched.

Then, suddenly, Rose snatched the bucket from Swiney's hand. She ran to the edge of the gully where the spring was. She tripped on a root and tumbled down the path, splashing into the water. She got right up, scooped a bucketful, and scrambled up the slippery, muddy path.

Swiney stood on the roof. He had taken off his shirt and was beating the fire with it.

"Quick, Rose!" he shouted. "Hand that bucket up. Hurry!" He squatted and leaned over the edge of the roof. It was low, but not low enough. The bucket was too heavy for Rose to lift all the way to Swiney's hand. A sob strangled her breath.

She poured some water out. Then she lifted the bucket with all her strength in both hands. Swiney barely caught the bail in his fingertips. He heaved the bucket onto the roof and poured the water all around the chimney. Steam and smoke mingled in the sunshine.

Rose peered inside the lean-to and sighed a great shivery sigh. There was no fire in the house. Only the roof had burned, and only a little. But the bread was ruined. Water ran down the outside of the stovepipe and into the stove, putting out the coals.

She slumped against the doorway and sat on the sill. She put her face in her hands. She began to shake all over. Then she cried.

Swiney sat down next to her. They sat there a long time, Rose crying and Swiney saying nothing. Finally Rose snuffled up the last of her tears. She wiped her face with the hem of her skirt.

"I better go," said Swiney.

Rose walked with him to Old Guts. Swiney climbed into the saddle and looked down at Rose. "You shouldn't cry none," he said. "It's all right now."

"Thank you," said Rose. "You saved our house. If you hadn't gone up on the roof . . ." The thought of what might have happened brought tears welling in her eyes again.

"I just climbed up the logs," Swiney said, grinning. Rose had to smile a little herself.

Now Rose waited for Mama and Papa with a dreadful sinking feeling. She was afraid she would cry when she tried to tell them about the fire. But she didn't.

"The roof caught fire from the stove," she said as soon as Mama and Papa rode close enough to hear. "But Swiney was here. He helped put it out."

Mama and Papa jumped from the horses at the same time, their faces lined with worry.

"What! How in the world . . ." Mama blurted. She looked at the roof. Then she looked inside the lean-to and inside the stove.

"Are you all right, Rose?" Papa asked.

Then Rose told Mama and Papa the whole story of that afternoon, except the part about feeding salt to the mules. She flushed hot with shame. She promised herself she would never do such a terrible thing again.

Mama bit her lip. Her eyes glimmered with tears, and she gave Rose a hug.

"It's my fault," Mama finally said. "Trying to save a little time by leaving that flimsy stove hot like that. The pipe sections must have come apart, letting the sparks get to the roof."

"Now, Bess, don't you fret so. It's just like your ma used to say, there's no loss without some gain. First thing, I'm going to tear down that old lean-to and build you a real kitchen, with a proper chimney."

THE NEW ROOM

The next day, Abe tore the lean-to away from the house. When they finished, there was nothing left but the hard bare ground and the doorway into the house. Papa and Abe began to build a new, bigger room on that spot, which would be the kitchen.

First they made a low stone wall foundation, in the shape of a large box. One side of the box was the log house.

On top of the foundation, they laid four, heavy squared-off logs of white oak. That was the sill. The sill must be good and sturdy to hold up the floor, the stove, and the walls. The stone foundation would keep the wooden sills from touching the ground, so they would stay dry and hard.

Next they laid heavy joists across the sill, to hold up the floor.

Then Abe helped Papa split logs into hewn clapboards to make the walls. The clapboards were rough like shingles. They weren't as fine and smooth as sawed boards. But Papa said, "Abe is a mighty fine wood cobbler. Those walls will stand as long as time lasts."

In no time at all, the walls were up and the roof was on. Papa left two square holes, one in the east wall and one in the west wall. He made two wooden shutters for those holes and hung them on leather hinges.

"In the fall, when it gets cold again, we'll get you proper glass windows," Papa told Mama. "But for now, while it's warm, we can leave the shutters open during the day when you want the light."

"It's just beautiful the way it is," said Mama, her eyes bright with pleasure.

There was a hole in the roof, too, for the

stovepipe. Papa lined the hole with tin, so the roof could never catch fire again.

Next Papa and Abe laid the floorboards on top of the heavy joists. The last board Papa laid was short, and it was in the middle of the floor. It was a trapdoor so Mama could pull it up and store vegetables and eggs in the cool space under the kitchen.

Then, the last thing, Papa took the old door from the house and fitted it to the doorway of the new room. The new kitchen was finished.

Mama and Rose swept all the dirt and sawdust off of the new floor. Then they moved the table from the house into the kitchen, and laid one of the rag rugs over the trapdoor. Papa gathered up his tools and began to put them away.

"What about the stove?" Mama asked. Papa had moved the stove outside while he and Abe built the new kitchen.

"It's getting late and I've got to feed and water the animals," said Papa. "The weather's good. Why don't you cook outside? We'll move the stove tomorrow, after breakfast."

"Very well," said Mama. "But it isn't a very

big job. It's just a small stove."

The next morning after breakfast, Papa said he had a load of fence rails to deliver in town. He was gone for several hours.

"I wonder what can be keeping him?" Mama said as she and Rose worked in the garden. "I've got my dough ready to bake. But I don't want to start a fire in the stove if we're going to move it."

Finally they heard the wagon splashing across the ford on Wolf Creek and rumbling up the hill. Fido raced down the wagon tracks to meet it. Papa had draped the oilcloth covers over something in the wagon-box, which rode low on its springs.

"I wonder what that could be," said Mama, mopping her forehead with the hem of her apron.

Papa drove right up to the kitchen's entrance. He set the brake and jumped down. A grin crinkled his mouth.

"I can see you've got something up your sleeve," Mama said. "What is it?"

Papa climbed into the wagon-box and

pulled off the oilcloth covers. Mama's mouth flew open. Sitting there, still half in its crate, was a brand-new cast-iron stove. Papa crossed his arms and waited for Mama to speak.

"Oh, Manly!" Mama cried out finally. Her hand flew to her mouth.

"It's got a hot water reservoir," Papa said proudly. "Now you can heat water and cook at the same time!"

The stove was beautiful. A pattern of sprigged flowers and leaves spread all over the doors. The nickel knobs and pins gleamed in the sunlight.

Rose waited for Mama's face to melt into happiness. But her mouth was tight, and her forehead furrowed. Finally she said, simply, "No."

Papa's eyes widened. "No?" he said.

"Yes," said Mama, more firmly this time. "I mean, no. I mean, you must take it back."

"What in tarnation?" Papa said.

"We cannot afford the expense," said Mama. "It's that simple. I couldn't bear to cook on it knowing we had gone further into debt for it. You will just have to take it back. I'm sorry. I know you only meant to please. But no. It's a sinful, wasteful extravagance for folks as poor as us."

Rose held her breath. She had never heard Mama speak so to Papa. Papa stared at Mama for a long moment.

"Dash it all, Bess!" he shouted suddenly. "Hang the expense. What's the difference if we owe an extra twenty dollars? If we can't pay it, Reynolds will give us more time. But I gave my word that I would buy this stove from him, and I don't aim to take it back."

Mama took a step back. "I just—" she began to say. But Papa's earnest voice drove on.

"See here," he said. "It's been more than fifteen years since I set out to find my fortune on the frontier. We can't live like sodbusters all our lives, letting the land grind us down year after year. I wouldn't wear out a dumb horse that way, not for any reason.

"Why should I let you wear yourself down, bending and slaving over a flimsy stove, worrying yourself half to death about fire? By jiminy, sometimes I . . ."

Then Papa took a big breath. "I've got work to do," he muttered. He turned and stalked off to the barn, forgetting to unhitch the team.

Rose had never seen Mama and Papa quarreling so. She had never heard Papa speak so forcefully.

Even the horses seemed stunned, standing still as statues. Fido looked at Rose, his head cocked in a question. Then he trotted off to the barn after Papa. The yard filled with a terrible silence.

A gloom thickened around Rose and pressed down on her. She yearned to go off somewhere where she could be alone and think. But she knew she shouldn't. Instead, she quietly followed Mama into the kitchen.

CHICKENS

D inner was dreadful. Mama and Papa did not speak to each other. Rose could not enjoy the beautiful new kitchen. Papa ate quickly and left to go work in the timber lot. Mama sighed after he had walked out the door.

"Well," Mama said after they had washed and dried the dishes. "It's time we cleaned out the henhouse. Two of the chickens have gone broody, and I think one of them has stolen her nest out somewhere. Maybe you can find it for me."

Rose was glad for the chore, for it was wonderful to be outside. Spring was hazy on the Ozark hills. The skeletons of the trees were covering themselves in leaves. The ground had finally begun to dry out, and the dust of the path was velvety cool to Rose's bare feet.

She called Fido to help look for the hen's nest. She looked in the bushes near the house first. Then she hunted around the outside of the barn, and under a pile of brush that was left from when the barn had been built in the fall. But she found no nest.

"Oh, well. She'll show up one of these days with her babies," said Mama. "She has never lost a single chick for me. And Fido is such a good dog, he will watch out for her as well."

Next they cleaned out the henhouse. They swept out all the dirty litter from the floor and emptied all the old straw out of the nest boxes that hung on the henhouse wall. Mama dabbed coal oil on the roosting perches and in the cracks in the walls of the henhouse to kill lice and mites.

Then they put down a blanket of fresh leaves, mixed with wood chips and sawdust. Mama showed Rose how to make sure each nest, now filled with fresh straw, had a cozy little hollow in the middle.

"It should be deep enough so the eggs won't roll off to the side and get cold," Mama explained. "But not so deep that a clumsy hen will step on the eggs and break them."

Then she set a white china doorknob in each of two nests. The hens would think they were eggs and lay their eggs in with them, instead of hiding them in the woods.

Rose thought chickens were not very smart and, except for roosters with their shimmering colored feathers, not pretty to look at. She couldn't play with them, or teach them tricks.

"Mama, why do you like chickens so well?" Rose asked. "They take so much care."

"A chicken is a miracle of nature," said Mama. "And the salvation of any farm. A hen asks very little: a dry, safe place to sleep at night, sunlight, fresh air, water, some mash every day, and a place to scratch for worms and bugs and grasshoppers.

"In return, she is a factory for food. She gives us eggs for nearly two years. She gives us young pullets to fry up for Sunday dinner. And when she is old and tired, she cooks into a delicious stew with dumplings.

"Just think of it: a good chicken will lay an egg every day. Now I have twenty hens. If they lay a dozen eggs each day, and Mr. Reynolds will give nine cents for the dozen, how much is that after a week?"

Rose was better at reading and writing than at arithmetic. She had to think a minute before she answered, "Sixty-two cents?"

"Sixty-three cents," Mama corrected. "Now, how much do you think that is after a month?"

That was too complicated a problem. "Two dollars and more than four bits. And in a year," Mama said, as she showed Rose how to multiply again by writing figures in the dirt, "that makes about thirty dollars."

Rose thought for a moment. Then she cried out, "Mama, that's more than the cost of the stove!"

The shadow of a frown flickered in Mama's blue eyes. Then she brushed away the numbers she had drawn in the dust.

"Yes, it is," she said. "But chickens are not predictable. They get sick, and remember last winter when that owl carried off my best layer? And besides, we have many other things to pay for.

"Well, never mind about that now. Let's get back to work on the garden. We need to get those fence rails up."

While they were working, Papa came back to the house with Abe. They climbed up into the wagon where it still stood by the porch.

Rose tried not to stare, but she couldn't help it. Papa and Abe slid the cast-iron stove out of the wagon and carried it into the kitchen.

Rose heard the sound of metal banging and hammering. After a time, the round chimney pipe poked through the roof hole. Rose stole sidelong glances at Mama, but Mama never looked up at the house. She just kept working, lifting fence rails and fitting them together.

When it was time for supper, Mama built a fire in the tin stove outside. Supper was almost as quiet as dinner had been. Only now, sitting in a corner of the kitchen was the shiny new stove.

After she had finished helping Mama with the dishes, Rose went to the barn to watch Papa doing his evening chores. He pitched fresh straw into the stables.

"How's my little prairie Rose tonight?" said Papa. "How do you like that new stove?"

Rose's face grew warm. She stammered from not knowing what to say.

"That's all right," said Papa, setting down the pitchfork. "I must have given you quite a fright, carrying on so. Were you scared?"

"A little," Rose said. "You never did that before."

"No, I never did," said Papa, his eyes wrinkling into a smile. "Hopefully never will again. Your mama's strong-willed, is all. Always was. Fact is, it's what I liked about her from the first. She's got spunk and spirit."

Then Papa looked at Rose with mirth in his eyes. "If you can keep it a secret, I'll tell you a nickname your grandpa used to call Mama."

"I can," Rose whispered loudly.

"Just between us?" he said.

"Yes!" Rose nearly squealed.

"Flutterbudget," Papa said.

"What?"

"Flutterbudget," said Papa again. "When your mama was young and she'd get her dander up, your grandpa teased her by calling her Flutterbudget."

Rose giggled. She thought it sounded a little like Mama. She liked it.

"All right, now," said Papa with a wink. "That's the last word on the subject."

"But can we keep the stove?" Rose asked.

"That's for Mama to decide," said Papa. "We must wait and see."

Rose walked back to the house. Just as she was about to walk into the kitchen, she heard the metal clank of a stove door closing. When she walked in, Mama was patting down her apron and looking around as if she had lost something.

"Here, Rose," she said, snatching the broom from its place in the corner. "Sweep out the kitchen. Then it's time for your lessons."

Rose's heart grew light. Having a secret with Papa made her feel grown-up. She understood that everything would turn out all right. And she knew that stove was here to stay.

THE FLOOD

The next day at dinner, Papa had a surprise. "How would you girls like to go fishing this afternoon?"

"Fishing?" Rose had never been.

"Abe says he knows a good spot up on Wolf Creek," said Papa. "I could do with some fresh fish for a change."

So Papa hitched the mares to the wagon, and they drove past the Kinnebrews' farm to pick up Abe and Swiney. Abe was carrying his fiddle.

"I thought you folks might fancy a bit of music to pass the while," he said.

"That would be wonderful," Mama said. So

as they drove out to Wolf Creek, Abe played a lively song with simple words they could learn right away.

> "Lark in the morning, sailing from her nest,
> Lark in the morning, sailing from her nest,
> Lark in the morning, sailing from her nest,
> Dew-drops falling from her snow-white breast.

> "The higher she flies, the sweeter she'll sing,
> The higher she flies, the sweeter she'll sing,
> The higher she flies, the sweeter she'll sing,
> And we'll all turn back to the green fields
> again."

Their voices rang out through the trees and blooming flowers.

Finally the road ran by a large, deep stream and the wagon stopped. That was Wolf Creek. Great tall trees lined the banks. Their tangled roots, like gnarled toes, stuck out of the mud at the water's edge.

In a swampy place next to the creek, Abe showed them where a grove of cane grew.

Swiney used his sharp knife to cut everyone cane stems to use as fishing poles.

Papa and Abe tied long pieces of heavy sewing thread on the ends of the canes. Close to the ends of the threads they tied little bits of wood. Then they tied hooks on the ends of the threads.

Swiney showed Rose how to find bait. They peeked under old rotting logs and found pale grubs, and slithery worms, and small slippery salamanders. Swiney took a worm and poked his hook through it. The worm squirmed and fought to get away, but it was stuck there.

"Here," Swiney said, giving Rose a worm. "Stick your hook in real good."

Rose tried, but the worm kept slithering away. It stretched and stretched until it was impossibly skinny. She jabbed at it, but the hook stuck her finger instead.

"Let me help you with that," said Papa. He took the worm in his hand, and with a flick of his fingers, the worm was wriggling on the hook.

Now they spread out along the bank to fish. Mama sat on an old log, pushed her bonnet back, and watched. "It's so peaceful here," she said. "I'm perfectly content to sit and enjoy it."

"Let's go upstream where that tree is hanging out over the water," Swiney suggested to Rose.

They sat out high over the water and dropped their lines into Wolf Creek. Rose could see the whole creek. She could see Abe and Papa fishing way downstream. In a shallow place, Fido was catching a fish that was trapped on a gravel bar. He grabbed it in his mouth and trotted off into the woods to eat it.

Rose could see the dark shadows of fish swimming in the creek. She could even see fish come to look at her hook. But none of them wanted it.

She looked out on the creek. A fallen log on the far bank was covered with turtles, lined up in a row, sunning themselves and catching flies.

Suddenly, right behind them on the bank, Rose heard a loud splash. A long, slinky brown creature climbed up on the mud. It had beautiful, shiny, wet fur on its arched back, and a pointed face, and whiskers. It shook itself like a dog. Then it looked around and scampered into the woods.

"What was that?" Rose asked.

"Mink," said Swiney. "He's scared the fish away."

But even as Swiney spoke, Rose felt a tug on her fishing pole. Then, all of a sudden, it nearly jumped out of her hands. She grabbed tight.

Her line slashed the water, this way and that. She could see the shadow of the fish. Its bright belly sparkled as it turned and fought the hook.

"I got one!" she shrieked.

She yanked on her pole, but that fish fought hard. The pole bent way over until she thought it might break.

"Don't jerk so hard!" Swiney shouted. "The hook will come out."

The fish fought and fought, but soon it tired and floated near the surface. Then Rose swung her pole over by the bank, where Swiney grabbed the line and unhooked it. It was a big fish with beautiful gold and blue scales and wide surprised-looking eyes. Swiney strung it through the gill on a piece of vine.

Rose ran downstream, carrying the still-flopping fish by the piece of vine. "Papa,

Mama, look!" she shouted.

"That will make good eating tonight," Papa said with a proud smile. Rose beamed. He took the fish and strung it with the fish he had caught. Rose counted. She and Papa had caught seven fish! And Abe had caught five fish for himself and Swiney. Swiney hadn't caught any.

Rose was proud as a gander. It made her feel good to help put food on their table.

They all fished a little while longer, but the fish had stopped biting. Finally Papa said it was time they got back to do chores.

Great piles of white clouds mounted in the hazy blue sky as they drove home. The air seemed to press down, hot and sticky.

"Looks like we might get some rain," said Mama. "We could use it. The garden is drying out."

"Most likely it'll be a gully-washer, too," said Abe. "I seen a couple snakes heading for high ground this morning. And the rocks in my corn patch was a-sweating dew. Them is sure signs a good rain is a-coming."

The sky darkened and the wind picked up

as they dropped Abe and Swiney off at the Kinnebrews'.

When they reached home, Papa unhitched the team and put the horses in the barn. Then he brought the mules in from the little pasture.

The sky closed in, shutting out the last rays of sunlight. The undersides of the dark clouds boiled. Thunder grumbled in the distance. Rose's heart beat with a strange excitement, and she felt feverishly hot.

"It smells like hail," Mama said. "Let's get the chickens inside."

She rattled a spoon in a bowl the way she always did at feeding time. Soon the yard was alive with scratching, quarreling, cackling chickens.

Rose helped Mama herd them into the henhouse. Just as the last chicken went in, Fido burst out barking from behind the large rock. A moment later, Mama's missing hen strutted into the yard, cackling loudly. Behind her, running to keep up, was a little parade of fluffy chicks, eleven in all. Behind them was Fido, herding them toward the henhouse!

"What a good dog!" Mama exclaimed. "The rain might have washed the poor things away. But the baby chicks are too little to sleep in the henhouse."

She caught the hen and put her in the wire coop with the little peeping chicks. Then Mama set the coop on top of some old newspapers she had laid down in the kitchen.

The first drops of rain spattered dark spots in the dust as Rose raced to bring in extra stove wood. Papa tipped the rain barrel over to dump out the old, stale water. Then he put it where it could catch rain running off the roof.

When the chores were done, they all went inside and shut the door. Fido turned around three times and curled up next to the stove.

Rose peeked out the glass window in the house. A tongue of lightning licked at Patterson's Hill, just across the valley. The thunder boomed loudly. It seemed caught among the hills, unable to escape, rolling and echoing. Then the rain came rushing down. It drummed loudly on the roof and poured off like water from a boot.

It beat so hard that Rose barely heard Mama

call her to help with supper. Then hail fell, rattling as though someone were throwing rocks on the roof. The wind howled through the trees. It clawed at the walls and rattled the shutters in the kitchen.

The wild sounds of the storm made Rose shiver. She wanted to climb into bed and pull the covers over her head.

"It's just a rainstorm, Rose," Mama nearly had to shout. "Come and help me clean these fish."

Mama cut off all the heads and showed Rose how to clean out the insides. Then she let Rose scrape the scales off the bass she had caught. The scales sparkled like jewels in the lamplight.

Mama sprinkled cornmeal on the cleaned pieces and fried them in drippings in the skillet. Then she fried the wild greens she had picked that day at Wolf Creek. The last thing she did was make a flour gravy to sop up with corn bread.

Finally they ate the delicious, delicate fish. It melted in Rose's mouth. She was hungry, and she ate and ate to fill the emptiness inside her.

The hail stopped and only rain pounded on

the roof all through supper. The dampness made the house stuffy. But the wind was blowing too hard to open the door or the shutters. They could hear broken branches and twigs rattling and sliding down the roof.

It was Saturday, so after dinner they took their baths. When Rose was finished, she went to look out the bedroom window. She rubbed a little clear spot in the fog that had collected on the glass. It was pitch-black outside, except now and then when a flash of lightning showed the trees bending and flailing in the wind.

Rose noticed a new sound, a roaring.

"What is that?" Rose asked.

Mama listened "It must be the spring, flooding from all the rain."

Just before bedtime, Papa lit the lantern and went to check the barn. It was still raining hard. When he came back, he had a worried look on his face.

"This is a bad storm," he said. "The whole ground is running like a river. There are a lot of tree limbs blown down. Fry Creek is over its banks."

They went to bed with an uneasy feeling. The rain lashed the window. The roaring of the spring and the creek was loud now. Rose was tired, but the drumming on the roof kept her awake.

She had just drifted off when the squeak of the lantern globe woke her up. Mama was looking out the window.

"Is it morning?" Rose asked.

"No," said Papa. "I heard a noise. I'm going to take a look."

Papa had been gone only a few moments when he came back in. His shoes were muddy and water poured off his hat. He shook himself like a sparrow.

"It's the henhouse," he said in a grim voice. "A tree fell on it."

"Oh, no!" cried Mama. "Is it bad?"

"I'm afraid so," said Papa. "We'll have to move them into the barn. Otherwise they may drown in this downpour, or catch a chill at the least."

"Get dressed, Rose," Mama said quickly.

Rose hurriedly pulled on her dress. Then she and Mama followed Papa out the door, into the driving rain and the inky blackness.

Big drops of rain stung her face, almost like bullets fired by the wind. In an instant, she was soaked to the skin.

She could feel mud squishing between her bare toes. The air smelled like newly plowed earth and freshly cut wood.

When the circle of lantern light fell on the henhouse, Rose gasped. The sturdy little henhouse was crushed in half. A tree trunk blocked the door. She could hear the chickens squawking inside.

Papa fetched the ax and two-handled saw from the barn. Rose held the lantern while he and Mama sawed the tree in half. When they had cut almost all the way through the trunk, there was a loud cracking sound. The trunk twisted and began to roll off the henhouse toward Mama.

Rose tried to shout, "Look out!" But the water ran off her hair, down her nose, and into her open mouth. Nothing came out.

"Watch it, Bess!" Papa shouted.

At the last moment, Mama jumped out of the way. The tree trunk splashed in the mud right at her feet. The henhouse walls sagged. Now it was not a henhouse anymore. It was an old pile of wet logs.

Papa and Mama began to pull loose logs away, one at a time. When they had made a hole in the pile of logs, Papa took the lantern and looked in. Over his shoulder Rose could see some chickens huddled in a pile.

Papa began to hand chickens out to Mama, one at a time. Mama gave the first two to Rose.

"Take these and wait for me," she said. The chickens were soaked and muddy and they smelled rank. They were too terrified to struggle or flap their wings. Rose took one in each arm. Then Mama took three in her arms, and Papa picked up three more.

Then he held up the lantern and they walked through the squishy mud and pools of water to the barn.

"We had best put them in the loft where they'll be safe and dry," Papa said when he got inside. He climbed partway up the ladder. Then Mama handed him the chickens and he set each one in the soft, dry hay.

Then they went back for more. They made three trips altogether. They saved seventeen of Mama's hens. The rooster was dead, and so were six of the young chickens.

"Thank goodness we kept the baby chicks inside," said Mama. "They never would have gotten through it."

When they were finished, they walked down the wagon tracks toward Fry Creek. Rose could not see into the blackness. But when they had walked only halfway, she heard a deep, terrifying roar. She noticed a wet, slapping, gurgling sound. Then, suddenly, her feet were in water!

"Mama! Papa! Look!" Rose cried out.

Fry Creek, which Rose could usually walk across in her bare feet, had climbed all that way up the wagon tracks toward the house. They stared into the darkness. All they could see in the lantern light was the black, rippling water. It lapped against the nearest tree trunks and foamed around the bushes. Rose could not picture it, but she knew the valley must be one great river!

Somewhere out in that horrible flood they heard the piteous bawling of a cow. Rose shivered.

"Do you think we're in any danger?" Mama shouted. "It's awfully high. Maybe we should move the livestock up the ridge."

"No," Papa said. "We're safe up here. But I better check on the neighbors when it's light. I reckon some of them will need help."

Visiting Alva

As soon as the first smudge of light showed in the window, Papa said, "If anybody needs a hand today, it'll be the folks downstream." Then he saddled one of the mules and rode off toward Kinnebrew's farm.

Mama and Rose went outside to look at the flooded land. Shattered tree limbs lay everywhere on the ground. It was still raining, though more gently now than during the night.

The henhouse was ruined, a pile of rubble. Mama fed and watered the chickens in the hallway of the barn.

The garden was all piles of mud and pools

of water. Here and there seed potatoes, their tender shoots sticking up, peeked out of the wet ground. A large limb had fallen on the fence and broken it down.

"I reckon we'll have to replant," Mama said with a weary sigh. "The potatoes will rot in this dampness. At least we have the tomato plants still in the hotbeds. We can plant them as soon as the soil dries out."

As Rose and Mama walked down the wagon tracks to the flood's edge, they noticed little brown toads everywhere. There were so many the earth seemed alive and moving.

At the flood's edge, water rippled around the tree trunks. Beyond the trees, they could see the brown plain of the flood. The swirling water was the color of dirty cream, spreading out as if poured from a pitcher. It boiled in places like stew.

"At least there isn't a drought anymore," Rose said, remembering the years of dry weather in South Dakota.

Mama chuckled. "Just think. Last summer we were choking on dust. Then the fires, and now this. As Papa says, if it isn't chickens, it's feathers."

The flood covered everything. You couldn't see an inch into the murky water. No one could ever cross it alive. Rose stared at the flowing water so long it made her dizzy. When she looked away the earth seemed to slide backward.

Across the flood, on the town side, some people were standing.

"It is the Cooleys!" said Mama. "They must have come to see how we are."

Mr. Cooley tried shouting. But they could not understand him over the sound of the flood. Now Rose could see Paul and George. She waved. Mama shouted back, "We're all right!"

But her voice was too small to reach. They all waved to one another, and then the Cooleys walked back to town.

Papa arrived home just before dinner. He told Rose and Mama that three of Mr. Kinnebrew's cows had died. But Mr. Kinnebrew gave Papa some of the freshly butchered beef as a thank-you, so at least some good came of it.

By suppertime, the flood had subsided. The creek was almost inside its banks, and the clouds parted in time for sunset.

As quickly as it had come, the flood was gone. The garden dried so quickly after the flood that the potatoes were saved from rotting.

Papa rebuilt the henhouse. Then he plowed a patch of new ground for corn. Rose helped plant the corn in the long furrows, four grains of corn together in each spot. When all the corn had been planted, Papa hitched a log sideways behind the mules. The log pushed the soil along, covering up the kernels.

Abe and Swiney did not come to help very often now. They were busy helping Mr. Kinnebrew plant and hoe his crops.

When the corn was laid by, Rose had more time to play. She often went for walks in the woods with Alva. Sometimes they waded in Fry Creek, capturing crayfish and finding tiny Indian arrowheads along the banks.

One morning Alva came to invite Rose to her house for dinner. Rose had never been to Alva's house and begged Mama to let her go.

"Very well," said Mama. "Remember your manners, and thank Mrs. Stubbins. I will expect you home in time for evening chores."

The Stubbinses' house was a log house, too. But it was very big, with two whole floors of rooms. On the porch were a spinning wheel and a loom. Under an oak tree stood a quilting frame. The week's washing hung in the morning sunshine.

Dozens of hens scratched in the yard, and ducks swam in a pond below the stone milk house. There was a summer kitchen, and a little smokehouse, and corncribs and cattle sheds, and a large ash hopper, and a pasture with a herd of beautiful Jersey cows, and horses and mules, too.

Rose had not known that Alva's family was so rich.

"Howdy, Rose," Mrs. Stubbins said heartily as she came out of the house. "We're right proud to welcome you. It's about time you was a-visiting."

A wisp of gray hair fell across Mrs. Stubbins's smiling face. Rose liked her very much. She remembered meeting her last fall when all the neighbors came to help Papa build the barn.

Dinner was a merry feast. She sat next to Alva at a long table with all of Alva's brothers and sisters, six in all, her mama and papa, and a hired hand. Mrs. Stubbins had fried a big plate of chicken and another plate of ham. There were boiled potatoes and hominy and biscuits with butter to spread on them. Rose couldn't remember when she had last had so many delicious foods at once.

"How do you find it here in the Ozarks?" asked Effie, Alva's oldest sister.

"I like it very much, thank you," Rose said politely. "Except for snakes and chiggers."

Everyone laughed good-naturedly.

"Yep, we got ourselves a mess of snakes and other pests in these hills," said Mr. Stubbins, spearing another piece of ham with his fork. "You young'uns got to watch out, running around barefoot all summer. Most snakes are harmless. But we got some that are right poisonous. Say, now, you ain't seen none of them hoop snakes about, have you?"

"No, sir," said Rose. "What kind of snake is that?"

Mr. Stubbins looked around the table with a twinkle in his eye. Effie giggled.

"Well, now," he said. "The hoop snake is one of God's strangest creatures. He only lives here in the Ozarks and not many folks has ever seed one.

"He climbs uphill like any sneaky old snake." Mr. Stubbins wriggled his arm to make it slither like a snake. "But when he wants to come back down the hill, he bites his tail in his mouth, makes himself into a wheel, and rolls down, just like a hoop.

"Now that old hoop snake is ornery. He likes to chase folks. The thing about it is, he's got a horn on his tail that is right sharp and mighty poisonous. Worse than a rattlesnake, or even a copperhead.

"His aim ain't too good, though. A hoop snake most always runs into a tree before he can hurt you. Then his horn gets stuck in the bark. And do you know what happens then?"

"What?" Rose said, her fork paused in midair.

"The leaves of that old tree curl right up, and in a few days, the tree dies."

Rose giggled uncertainly. Mrs. Stubbins rolled her eyes and got up to clear the dishes. Rose looked at Alva, but Alva was looking at her father with wondering eyes.

Rose began to pick up plates to help with the dishes.

"You ain't got to do that," said Alva. "My sisters do the washing up. Come on. I'll show you around our farm."

Rose thought Alva was very lucky to have big sisters to help with the chores. At home Rose helped with everything. She was almost as busy as Mama, all day long.

Alva and Rose went into Mr. Stubbins's great barn and played with the baby calves. Alva showed Rose how to milk a cow, but Rose's hands weren't strong enough to make the milk come out.

They found one of the barn cats nursing her kittens in a hollow place in the hay. The kittens were as tiny as mice. They paddled around with their little paws and sucked at their mother's stomach.

"When they get older, you can have one if you want, Rose," said Alva.

"Could I?" Rose nearly shouted.

"Pa said we got too many cats," Alva said. "Which one you want?"

They all looked the same, with softly striped orange fur on their backs and velvety white fur on their bellies. Their short, pointy tails stood straight up and trembled as they nursed. Only one had a black foot, and it was a little smaller than the rest.

"That one," said Rose. "I like that one because I can tell it from the others." She decided she would call it Blackfoot.

"I'll tell Pa and when he says it's old enough, you can come and take it," Alva said.

Rose clapped her hands with joy. "Thank you, Alva! Thank you so much."

They played away the rest of that afternoon. They made a little dam in the branch of the spring and watched the water spiders darting on the water's surface. They made mud pies and left them to bake in the warm sun.

Then it was time for Rose to go home. She ran most of the way, full of excitement. She skimmed bushes and leaped over stumps. She laughed out loud when a frog she had startled *kerplunk*ed into Fry Creek.

But when she got close to home, she slowed down and walked. And she thought. It had been a wonderful day. She was very happy about her kitten. But a part of Rose felt hollow. She liked Alva's family. She had enjoyed all those people around to listen to and talk with.

Rose wished she had brothers and sisters to play with. She imagined how wonderful it must be to live at Alva's house, to be Alva and have so many wonderful things to do every day. Rose wished Mama and Papa had a cow, so she could have milk to drink and butter for her bread.

Then she blushed hot with shame at her thoughts. But she could not stop from having them.

Soon it would be a whole year since Rose's family had left Dakota. Yet Rose could see it would be a long while before Rocky Ridge Farm looked anything like Mr. Stubbins's wonderful farm. When the apple trees came into bearing, they would have everything they ever wanted. But that was years and years away. Rose did not know how she could ever stand the wait.

OFF TO SCHOOL

R ose told Mama all about her wonderful afternoon and Blackfoot as Mama finished ironing Rose's new dress.

"We certainly could use a good mouser," Mama said, changing the iron for a freshly hot one that sat on the stove. "When we get the crops in this fall, we will need a cat to keep the rats and mice out of the corn and oats.

"There," she said, holding up the dress. "All done. Let's put it on you so I can pin the hem."

Rose wriggled into the new blue-and-lavender gingham. The cloth was stiff with ironing and newness.

"Your hands are soiled," Mama said. "Try to keep them away from the cloth." She stepped back to look at Rose, chin in hand. "That was a good choice you made. The blue matches your eyes. You look very pretty in it."

Mama's eyes shone as she looked. Rose smiled happily. She couldn't wait for a chance to wear her new dress.

She stood on a chair so Mama could pin up the hem. Rose was quiet for a moment as Mama worked. Then she asked, "Mama, can we have a baby brother, or a baby sister?"

Mama stopped pinning and looked at Rose with searching eyes. A shadow seemed to pass across her face, and then she sighed.

"I don't think so, sweetheart," she said softly. "Are you lonesome?"

"A little, sometimes," said Rose. "Why can't we have a baby? God brings babies to everyone else."

Mama sat down at the table and asked Rose to sit, too. "Do you remember, when you were a baby, when Papa and I were sick and you stayed with Grandma?"

"A little, I think," Rose said.

"And do you remember right after that, the baby boy we had in South Dakota who died before we could give him his name?"

"Yes," Rose said in her smallest voice.

"Well, Papa and I wanted to have another baby, and we prayed for another baby. But I think that when I was sick, God decided we wouldn't have one. Do you understand?"

"I think so," said Rose. "But . . . why does God bring babies to some people and not to us?"

"God brought you, Rose. That was the greatest gift of all for Papa and me. To have you is enough, if that is His will. No one can know why God decides anything.

"And as for feeling lonesome, you won't be for long," Mama said. "School starts next week. Just think of the friends you'll make!"

Rose's mouth flew open to speak, but nothing came out. She had not thought about school for a long time.

The first day of school, Rose had to get up early to have time for all her chores before breakfast. As soon as breakfast was done, she helped Mama wash the dishes.

Finally, she put on her new dress and pinafore. Mama plaited Rose's hair tightly into two braids and tied on Rose's yellow hair ribbons.

Then Mama took out of the trunk her old copy of *McGuffey's Third Eclectic Reader*. Mama had been a schoolteacher. While Rose was waiting to start school, Mama had taught the lessons at home using her old textbooks. Rose was all the way through the Third Reader, and she knew it practically by heart.

Mama gave Rose her slate and a new slate pencil. Then she handed Rose her dinner pail.

"There's a surprise in it for you," Mama said. "Don't you peek or nibble before Teacher calls dinner. Promise?"

"I promise," said Rose. Now she was ready. Mama kissed Rose and watched from the porch as she walked down the wagon tracks toward Fry Creek. Fido bounded alongside her, but Mama whistled for him to come back. Fido looked at Rose and cocked his head. Mama whistled again and he scampered away, back up the hill. Rose waded across the creek, holding up the hem of her dress so it wouldn't get wet. The cool water tingled on her bare feet and washed away the dust.

The footpath that went over Patterson's Hill started on the other side. Rose trudged up the hill past Williams Cave, where she had explored with Alva. The sun was already high, and the air was shimmery warm. Rose pushed her sunbonnet back off her head.

Finally she reached the top of Patterson's Hill, from which she could see the back of the tall, brick schoolhouse. Children were walking up the road from town. Other children were playing on the bare ground to the side. Rose looked for Paul and George, but she did not see them.

Suddenly she realized that she was really going to school. Something churned in her stomach. She had loved her old school in South Dakota, but wasn't at all sure she would like school here in Missouri.

New Girl

R ose walked slowly down the slope toward the school. Her heart pounded in her chest. Just then the bell began to ring, and all the children raced toward the front door. Rose hurried not to be last.

Then she was in a crowd of children who were pushing, jostling, and laughing. At the head of the crowd, children were pouring through the big double doors. Rose caught a glimpse of Paul as he was swallowed up by the doors.

Finally Rose reached the entryway. She stood just inside the door, not knowing which way to turn. A stream of children poured in around her. A tall bald man with a long beard called out, "You there, little girl in the plaid. What reader are you in?"

Rose didn't know what to say. Then the man saw her book. He pointed, "Third Reader, to the right."

Rose walked through another door. A boy rushed past her, knocking her dinner pail to the floor. She picked it up and looked around. The room was full of double desks, four rows of four desks. The floor was bright yellow wood and shiny. The room smelled of linseed oil.

There were many great, tall windows on three of the walls, and a large heating stove. The opposite wall from the stove was partly painted black. That was the blackboard. All the other walls were painted a pale sickly green.

Rose stood uncertainly next to the wall by the door. It seemed every seat was taken. Then she spotted an empty one at the front, next to a girl with beautiful, curly black hair falling in ringlets. She wore a lovely lawn dress and shiny black shoes. Rose liked to sit in the front, so she went to that desk. But when she put her book and slate down on the desktop, the little girl turned and frowned at her.

"You can't sit here," she said quickly. "It's my friend's seat. She's coming in a minute."

Rose flushed hot. She stood in front of all those desks of strangers, not knowing what to do or where to go. Several children were staring at her. Two girls sitting together whispered to each other and pointed at her.

Finally Rose spied an empty desk in the back row. She almost ran down the aisle and quickly sat in one of the seats. She was relieved to be where no one could stare at her.

Then Rose looked at her seatmate. Her head was resting on her hands on the desk, her face turned the other way. Rose couldn't tell if she was resting or sleeping. Her faded brown calico dress had a large patch of gingham sewn on the front. Her brown hair fell limp and unbraided over her shoulders. Her feet were dirty. Then she sniffled loudly.

Now the teacher began to speak.

"My name is Professor Kay," the man said. He wrote his name on the blackboard in chalk.

Then he took the roll. He called out many names. "Blanche Coday," he called out.

The girl with the beautiful black hair called out, "Present, sir." Her seatmate was very pretty, too. Her blond hair hung in a silky braid down her back. Her white dimity dress had a butterfly pattern on it, and a gold bracelet hung around her wrist.

Rose listened anxiously so she wouldn't miss her turn. One by one, the students answered to their names. Her throat grew so choked with expecting to speak that she could hardly breathe. Finally, all the names were called, including Irene Strong, the snuffling girl sitting next to Rose. All the names had been called except Rose's.

"Is there any scholar here whose name I did not call?"

Rose raised her hand.

"Stand up, please," Professor Kay said. He pointed a long stick at her. Everyone in the room turned to look at Rose. Her neck blazed hot under all those eyes. "What is your name, please?"

"Rose Wilder," Rose whispered.

"Speak up. I can't hear you." Titters rippled around the room.

Rose said her name again.

"Very well," Professor Kay said, writing it down. "Be seated."

The desk seat was too tall. Rose's legs already ached from dangling. The room was stifling hot. A trickle of sweat ran down the back of her neck.

Now Rose had only one thought in her mind, to run out of that school and all the way home. But she did not budge from her seat. She was too shy to run away.

Then the lessons began with recitations. Professor Kay called on the boys first.

Harry Carnall, a boy in overalls, stood up and read slowly from his reader, "'George's mother was very poor. 'Stead of havin' bright blazin' fahrs in winter, she had nothin' to burn . . .'"

"Ing!" Professor Kay barked. "No-*thing*." He stood up and wrote on the blackboard, *having, blazing,* and *nothing*. After *nothing*, he wrote ten times: *ing, ing, ing*.

He turned around, folded his arms across his chest, and glared at Harry Carnall.

Harry giggled nervously and looked around at the other boys. Professor Kay just stared at him. Finally Harry said, "What's the *ing, ing, ing* doin' up thar a whole passel of times?"

"I am glad you asked that question," Professor Kay said. "I wrote the *ing* up there ten times so you won't forget it. I have hardly heard anyone pronounce *ing* since I came to this school last winter. We are going to learn it now. Let us all say *ing* together, ten times."

Everyone sang out a chorus of *ing*s. All those *ing*s together sounded like a pondful of spring peepers. Rose kept her mouth shut. She did not need to learn how to pronounce *ing*. The lesson was stupid.

Everyone took turns reciting. Rose grew bored. She was the last to take a turn.

"Recite, please, the first two paragraphs of 'Johnny's First Snowstorm.'"

Rose knew her whole book almost by heart. She recited easily:

"Johnny Reed was a little boy who never had seen a snowstorm till he was six years old. Before this, he had lived in a warm country, where the sun shines down on beautiful orange groves, and fields always sweet with flowers.

"But now he had come to visit his grandmother who lived where the snow falls in winter. Johnny was standing at the window when the snow came down."

"Very well done," Professor Kay said. "Please be seated."

Rose knew she should have been pleased with her teacher's praise, but she didn't care. She knew all of her Third Reader. She had even read the Fourth and Fifth Reader, as well.

So she sat there, legs aching, prickly hot, looking at the ugly green walls and watching Professor Kay. He carried a long stick that he poked down the back of his soiled shirt to scratch himself.

Finally Professor Kay rang a tiny bell that he kept on his desk. That meant to put books away.

He rang it a second time for everyone to stand up. The third time he rang, it was dismissal.

Rose raced outside with all the other children and waited by the doors for Paul and George. Paul came clomping noisily down the stairs with two other boys. His face lit up in a wonderful way when he saw Rose. His bright smile was like the sun coming up.

"Hey, Rose!" he shouted. "Finally came to school, huh?"

"Yes," said Rose cheerfully. "But I don't like it very much. I wish I could be upstairs where you are."

"It's not so bad," he said. "At least you don't have to stay home and do chores. And then you can play at recess and dinnertime."

All the boys were racing around to the boys' side of the schoolhouse to play a game.

"See you later, Rose!" Paul shouted. Then he dashed off to follow them.

George came out of the schoolhouse next. He shouted hello to Rose and ran off to play with the other boys.

Rose was by herself. A group of town girls in

pretty dresses, including Blanche Coday, were playing house with some rocks. But they did not invite Rose to join them and she was too shy to ask.

Some other children were playing crack the whip. But Rose's spirits were so low, she did not feel like joining. She looked longingly at the crest of the hill that stood between her and home.

Recess was over in fifteen minutes. The bell rang and all the children crowded through the door again. The rest of the morning dragged on. Rose stared out the window at the trees rustling in the breeze. She wondered what Alva was doing today. Probably she was helping her papa bring in the hay, or playing with the kittens, or just about anything that was more fun than sitting in that stuffy schoolroom.

AFTERNOON LESSONS

At noon, Paul and George went back to the hotel to eat dinner. Rose ate by herself under a tree at the edge of the playground.

In her molasses tin, she found two pieces of brown bread with bacon fat spread on them, a boiled potato, and a dried-apple turnover. That was Mama's surprise.

Rose ate the turnover first. The sweet, crisp taste melted in her mouth. Eating it made her feel a bit better. Then she slowly ate her bread and the potato. Two girls who were twins sat near her. They were dressed exactly the same, in sprigged green calico. Out of their large tin they each took a piece of fried chicken and a biscuit.

"You're a new girl, aren't you?" one of the twins said. "Come and eat with us. We like to meet new girls."

"Thank you," Rose said gratefully. She picked up her things and sat down next to the twins.

"My name is Dora," one of the girls said. "This is my sister, Cora. We're the Hibbard twins. What's your name?"

"Rose Wilder," said Rose. "I'm in the Third Reader. This is my first day in school. I used to live in South Dakota."

"I know where that is," Cora said proudly. "It's very far. All the way north. Almost to Canada."

Rose thought Dora and Cora were like one person split in half. Even their voices were exactly the same. She wondered how anyone could tell them apart.

"The first day of school is so much fun," said Dora. "We like to see our friends again, and everyone is so excited."

"I liked school in South Dakota, but I don't like it very much here," said Rose. "The girls are not very friendly. I mean, except for you.

And the teacher is a man. I like a woman teacher better."

"So do we!" Cora said cheerfully. "We like our teacher, Miss Pimberton, so very much."

Rose chatted with the Hibbard twins until they had finished their dinner. Then they all joined some other girls who were playing cat and mouse.

Rose liked cat and mouse. The sound of other children giggling and shouting, and the excitement of all that running and shrieking, cheered her up. When it was her turn to be mouse, her legs rejoiced to be running and free. Soon she was laughing as hard as anyone else.

When the bell rang for afternoon books, Rose said good-bye to Cora and Dora. On her way inside, Rose wondered what it would be like to have a sister who looked and sounded exactly like her. Twins were lucky, she decided. They always had a best friend to play with.

Rose took her seat and the afternoon passed just as the morning had. She knew all the answers to Professor Kay's questions and was soon bored.

After recess was spelling. Spelling was Rose's best exercise. Professor Kay drew a long, straight chalk mark on the floor at the front of the classroom. Everyone stood on it in a line, in alphabetical order, facing Professor Kay. Rose's name was last. She must start at the foot of the line. Then the teacher called out words and each student took a turn spelling, beginning with the person at the head of the line.

"*Frequently,*" Professor Kay said when it was Rose's turn.

"*Frequently,*" Rose repeated. "F-r-e, *fre,* q-u-e-n-t, *quent, frequent,* l-y *ly, frequently.*"

Rose felt a tingle of excitement every time she got a word someone had misspelled and she could move up one place in line. All afternoon they spelled. Rose moved up the line, closer and closer to the head, closer to Blanche Coday, the girl who wouldn't let Rose sit with her. Blanche was a good speller, and she had spelled down the two boys who were ahead of her.

Finally Rose stood next to Blanche and Rose was only one word away from being the best speller in the class that day. Her stomach quivered, her hands were cold, and her palms were damp. She wanted more than anything to spell down Blanche Coday.

But every word Professor Kay gave Blanche she spelled correctly: *curious, purpose, material, cautiously*. Every time she got one right, Blanche looked at Rose smugly. But every word Professor Kay gave Rose, Rose spelled correctly as well: *reminded, including, constructed*.

The next time it was Blanche's turn, Professor Kay said, *"Chiefly."*

"Chiefly," Blanche said, tossing her head so her curls shook. "C-h-e-i-f, *chief*." Rose trembled with joy. "L-y *ly*, *chiefly*."

It was everything Rose could do to keep still. She knew by heart the rule "'I' before 'e,' except after 'c.'" Blanche had got it wrong! Rose's whole body poised to pounce on that word.

"That is wrong," said Professor Kay. "Next."

Blanche shot a hard, pinched look at Rose.

"Chiefly," Rose said with confidence. "C-h-i-e-f, *chief*, l-y, *ly*, *chiefly*."

"Very good," said Professor Kay. He wrote

Rose's name on a corner of the blackboard and put a mark next to it. That was a headmark, for Rose had gotten to the head of the line by turning down all the other scholars.

"That will be all for today. Class is dismissed."

Everyone scrambled to leave. Rose picked up her book, her slate, and her molasses tin, and bounded out of school. Girls like Blanche might laugh at her, but she could beat any of them in spelling. She flew home, running down Patterson's Hill and splashing carelessly across Fry Creek.

Fido ran down the wagon tracks to meet her, barking with joy. Rose was never so happy to see him, and Mama, too, when she came to the kitchen door, drying her hands on her apron.

So much had happened that day that Rose didn't know where to start the telling.

"First things first," Mama said. "Change your dress and do your chores. You can tell us all about school when we sit down to eat."

With a sigh, Rose did as she was told. She took off her school dress and hung it up carefully. Then she completed her after-school chores and washed her hands and face and set the table. Finally Papa came in to wash up. It was wonderful to be home.

She told Mama and Papa that the town girls in her reader were very pretty but they were rude. She didn't like Professor Kay very well, either.

"He's dirty and he's the stupidest teacher in the world," Rose complained. She knew it was wicked to say, but all her feelings from that day just came tumbling out before she could stop them. "And he gives the stupidest lessons: '*ing, ing, ing.*'"

"That's enough of such talk, Rose," Mama said firmly. "Besides, people aren't stupid. They are just more or less foolish."

"He is more and more foolish," Rose said. Papa chuckled, but then stopped when he saw that Mama was not smiling.

"The lessons are dull," Rose complained. "I know them all. I know all the spelling words, too. I made head in spelling."

"That's very good," Mama said. "I'm proud of you."

But Rose did not feel proud. It had been too easy.

"You must have seen Paul and George," Papa said. "How are they doing?"

"I saw them," said Rose. "But they are in the Fourth Reader, on the second floor. At recess, they play with the boys. They go to the hotel for dinner."

As they ate supper, Rose told Mama and Papa about the Hibbard twins and about playing cat and mouse.

After that, Rose fell silent in thought. Mama did not understand how unhappy she was in school. Rose could not bear another day staring at those walls and watching Professor Kay scratch himself. She simply couldn't.

When they were done eating, Rose finally screwed up her courage to ask, "Do I have to go back? Can't I stay home and study my lessons here, like before?"

"Why, Rose, it's only the first day!" Mama said, getting up to clear the dishes. "You mustn't give up so easily. In time, the other students will catch up to you, you will make some friends, and then it will be more fun."

Rose frowned.

"Don't pout," said Mama. "What must be done is best done cheerfully."

In Trouble

Rose dawdled so long on the way to school the next morning that she was the last to take her seat. At recess, she watched Paul and George and the other boys playing. Morning recitation dragged on, and Rose stared out the window.

She was thinking about Alva and Blackfoot when she heard her name.

"Rose Wilder!" Professor Kay called out impatiently. "I said, please rise and recite."

Rose sprang to her feet, knocking her reader to the floor with a *thud*. Blanche chortled and some of the other children giggled. Rose's cheeks burned hot.

She picked up her book. "I . . . I'm sorry," she said. "I lost my place."

"Please recite the first three paragraphs on page thirty-one, 'The Beaver.'"

Rose found her place and recited those paragraphs perfectly.

Noon finally came. Rose dashed outside and wolfed down her dinner in nothing flat. When she was done she put her tin back on the shelf in the classroom. Then Rose left school. She had decided to visit her new kitten.

She ran all the way to the Stubbinses' farm. She must hurry to have time enough to get back before afternoon books. Alva was just coming out of her house from dinner.

"How come you ain't in school?" Alva asked.

"I am," said Rose. "I just wanted to see Blackfoot."

"Come on, then," Alva said. "The kittens' little eyes are open now."

The kittens had grown so in just a few days! Now they played together, gnawing one another's ears and tails, pouncing, and kicking with their tiny back feet. Rose and Alva laughed at how comical they were.

Rose picked up Blackfoot. He climbed up her pinafore onto her shoulder. He sniffed tiny breaths that tickled in her ear, and batted at her hair ribbon. Then he mewed softly to get down.

"Oh, Alva," Rose said, "I hate school so."

"I'm glad my ma and pa don't make me go to no school," said Alva. "My pa says you don't need no schooling to know how to milk cows and hoe corn."

Then they left the kittens and walked out into the yard to get a drink at the spring.

"Look, Rose!" Alva shouted. "Bees are drinking water. Let's follow them and see if we can find the nest."

"I don't think I ought to," said Rose. "I might be late for afternoon books."

"We won't go far," Alva insisted. "Come on, there goes one now."

Alva took off running and Rose followed. "I can still see it!" Alva shouted. They ran through the woods, a long way. Rose could never see the bee, but Alva kept shouting,

"There it is! Hurry up, Rose!"

But then she lost sight of it. "It don't matter, anyway," Alva said. "'A hive in May is worth a load of hay, but a hive in July ain't worth a fly.'"

On the way back, they stopped to watch two colts racing each other back and forth across the field. Then they hunted quail nests along the fence. They found a blackberry patch. Alva took a stick and beat the bushes first, to scare away snakes. Then they plucked and ate all the ripe berries they could find.

Rose remembered school, but she was sure she still had time to get back for afternoon books. She had not heard the bell, and it wasn't so far if she ran.

Along the spring branch, they hunted crayfish. Then they built a dam and watched a little pond form behind it.

Finally Rose said she had better go. She ran all the way back to school. When she got to the top of Patterson's Hill, Rose gasped. The schoolyard was empty! Her stomach flip-flopped.

The next thing she noticed made her heart skip a beat. There was a wagon standing by the front of the school. She recognized Pet and May, Papa's horses.

A great weight settled around Rose's shoulders. She walked very slowly down the hill and climbed the steps, one at a time. Her feet were as heavy as stones.

Then she stood in the schoolroom doorway. Mama was sitting in a desk with her back to the door. Papa stood next to her. Professor Kay looked up at Rose from his desk. He nodded toward her and looked at Mama with raised eyebrows. Mama turned and looked at Rose. Her mouth was tight and her eyes glared fiercely.

Professor Kay cleared his throat. "I best be going," he said. "I expect you have the matter in hand now."

Then he left without another word.

"Where have you been?" Mama asked sternly. Her voice had never had such a hard edge.

Rose could think of nothing to say. She stared at the floor.

"I asked you a question," Mama said. "You weren't in school all afternoon, and Professor Kay dismissed class an hour ago. Papa and I have been worried sick. *Where have you been?*"

Rose flinched.

"I went to Alva's," Rose said meekly. "I'm sorry, Mama. I only wanted to see the kitten. I didn't know it would be so long."

Mama said, "To think you could have been lying hurt somewhere and Papa and I with no idea where to begin to look. I can't imagine where you got it into your head . . ."

"Now, Bess," Papa interrupted. "She's here now, safe and sound. Just some childish foolishness. But you mustn't ever do anything like that again, Rose."

"Yes, Papa," Rose said softly.

Mama said, "We have told Professor Kay to keep you in during recess and dinner as many days as he sees fit, until you have learned your lesson. You must obey him the same as you obey Papa and me."

"Yes, Mama," said Rose, trying to hold back tears. She hated causing Mama and Papa to worry.

Every day for the rest of that week, Professor Kay kept Rose inside during recess and dinner.

At first, it was torture to be still and listen to the high, light voices of the other children playing outside.

But Professor Kay chatted pleasantly with Rose while they ate their dinners.

"You are a very good student, Rose," he said. "I don't blame you much for being bored. By rights, you ought to be in the Fourth Reader. Your mother taught you well."

"Thank you," said Rose, a little surprised at how nicely Professor Kay was treating her.

Rose screwed up her courage. "Could I go into the Fourth Reader, Professor Kay? I promise I would be good and study hard to keep up."

"I am sure you would, and I wish I could say yes," Professor Kay said. "But Miss Pimberton's room is full and you are a bit young for her class. I'll tell you what, though. There is a library of books in her room that have been donated to the school. If you wish, you may pick one out to read. Would you like that?"

"Yes, sir," Rose said. "I would like it very much. Thank you."

When they were done eating, they walked

upstairs to Miss Pimberton's room. In the corner was a bookcase with four shelves. Two of the shelves were almost full of books.

Rose had never seen so many books. There were books of poems, storybooks, and important-sounding books, like *Pride and Prejudice* and *The House of the Seven Gables.*

Rose couldn't decide on just one. She wanted to read them all, to learn the secrets hidden in all those hundreds of pages of words. Finally she picked a big book called *The Leatherstocking Tales.* It had been written by a man named James Fenimore Cooper many years before. Rose picked it because she liked the title. Professor Kay said it was a book of stories about the beginnings of America.

At noon the next day, Rose sat at her desk, ate her dinner as quickly as she could, and read. She began at the beginning. She did not understand some of it, and there were quite a few words she had to ask Professor Kay to explain.

But the more Rose read, the more she wanted to read. It was very pleasant to sit quietly in the empty classroom. In no time at all she was carried away from school. She was tramping through the winter snows of New York many years ago, hunting deer with a smoothbore rifle, and wearing a deerskin coat with the hair still on.

When the bell rang for afternoon lessons, she hated to put the book down. Rose thought the people in books were more real than the people she saw every day.

In the afternoon each day, there was spelling. Every day Rose started at the foot and ended at the head. She always turned down Blanche Coday.

On Friday, Professor Kay let Rose take the book home with her. On Saturday night and Sunday afternoon, Mama read aloud from it to Rose and Papa.

On Monday, Rose took *The Leatherstocking Tales* back to school. Her punishment was ended and she could go out with the other children. But she would still read it. She propped herself up against a tree at the edge of the schoolyard and opened the book on her knees.

But before she could sit down to read, she

had a chore Professor Kay had given her. He asked Rose to clean the erasers. That was a special chore that he only gave to the best students. Rose was surprised that after she had been disobedient, he would give her a special chore. But she was even more surprised when Professor Kay picked Blanche Coday to help her.

At dinnertime, she and Blanche took two erasers each and walked quietly to the edge of the playground. They clapped the erasers together to get out all the chalk dust. They did not speak a word to each other.

The next day, as they were clapping the chalk dust out of the erasers, Blanche startled Rose by asking her in a haughty voice, "Where are you from? You aren't from around here. Anyone can see that. You don't talk like girls from around here."

"My mama and papa brought me here from South Dakota," Rose said. "We drove last summer in a covered wagon all the way."

Blanche clapped her erasers a few more times. Then she said, "You haven't been in school here before. How did you learn so many spelling words?"

"My mama taught me," said Rose. She did not like the tone of Blanche's voice, but she tried to be polite anyway. "She was a school-teacher once. I like to read, too. I learned many words from reading books."

"Well, anyone can see that plain as day," Blanche said tartly. "It's all you do, read and stare out the window and be teacher's pet. But don't think we can be friends just because you are so smart. After all, you're a country girl."

With that, Blanche flounced off to return her erasers. Rose's face stung as though it had been slapped. Alva was right, Rose thought angrily. Town girls are stuck up.

Rose decided then and there that she would never, ever let Blanche Coday spell her down.

SUMMER

Every day in spelling, Rose turned down Blanche and ended up at the head of the line. And Rose remembered each time her promise to herself and studied her spelling harder.

Irene took sick and stopped coming to school. Irene's older sister said Irene had caught diphtheria. The word echoed in Rose's mind like a thunderclap. That was the terrible illness Mama and Papa had once had.

The whole family could not leave their house because they were quarantined. Only Irene's sister could go out to school and to town on errands. But she said she must sleep in the barn, so she would not catch it, too.

Rose was friendly with Dora and Cora and some of the other students, but she did not make a best friend at school. She did not fit in with the town girls, or the other country girls.

Even so, she was mostly content. She had grown to like Professor Kay. She enjoyed watching Paul and the older boys playing two-cornered cat. And Rose had been an only child all her life. She was used to pleasing herself.

At home, the whole farm was growing. The garden was rows and rows of different shades of green. There were radishes, lettuce, onions, carrots, and tomatoes.

The corn had sprung up almost overnight. Already the stalks reached Rose's waist.

In the same soil with the corn, Papa had planted the pole beans. The thin tendrils of their stems trailed along the ground, crawling straight to the corn. Then they hugged the cornstalks and began to climb them. The cornstalks were the poles. Before Rose helped pick the corn in the fall, the beans would be ready to harvest. That was a way to get two crops out of one piece of ground. Rose wondered how the beans knew to climb the cornstalks.

In the orchard, the young apple trees were filling in with new growth. Slender, bright green fingers reached out from the end of each gray branch and twig. Papa brought home wagonloads of wood ashes from town and spread some around each tree. The ashes would sweeten the soil and keep away wood-eating bugs that might hurt the trees.

One Sunday, Alva came by with Blackfoot. He immediately rubbed against Rose's leg.

"He remembers me!" she cried. Blackfoot was even more beautiful than she recalled. And he had grown so big. His short, straight tail had become long and wavy.

When Fido came to sniff at him, the kitten batted the dog's nose playfully. Fido gave a short, surprised bark that sent Blackfoot skittering behind Rose. But in a moment, he came back out, sat down, and licked his paw, keeping his bright eyes on Fido. Soon after that, they became friends and even played together.

Summer flowed on, slow, lazy, and stifling hot. Specks of dust hung in the still air, catching the sunlight and shimmering in the heat. The hot weather pressed down like an iron pot lid.

One night at supper Papa said, "It's too blamed hot for cutting wood. Why don't we gather up some folks and throw ourselves a picnic?"

"That would be lovely," said Mama. "We've been so busy. We could all do with a change of scene. Do you think the Cooleys would come?"

"Don't see why not," said Papa. "I'll ask them when I'm in town tomorrow."

"Perhaps we could ask the Kinnebrews, as well," Mama suggested. "We haven't all met them yet."

In a day, it was decided. The three families would meet on the Ava Road south of town and drive down to Bryant Creek.

The morning of the picnic, they hurriedly did their chores, ate a cold breakfast, and loaded the wagon. Papa pitched a pile of hay in the back to sit on and for the horses to munch. The picnic food was packed in a basket with a clean white towel tucked over it. A jug of sweetened ginger water sat under the wagon seat.

Then they were off in the first gray light of dawn. When they met up with the Kinnebrews and the Cooleys, there were many shouts of hello, and they drove off into the fresh morning. Rose tingled with excitement to be going somewhere different, and to have a day away from school.

Finally, when Rose was getting fidgety and the air was turning muggy, they came to a wide stream, bigger than Wolf Creek. That was Bryant Creek.

They set themselves up on a gravel bar, right next to the water. Rose helped Paul and George gather wood for a fire.

Mr. and Mrs. Kinnebrew had brought two big watermelons for everyone to eat at dinner. Rose's mouth watered just looking at them. Their two sons, Coley and Claude, carried them to the creek's edge and set them in a quiet pool to chill. They weighted the watermelons down with stones to keep them from floating away. Mr. Kinnebrew scolded the boys to quit fighting over how to pile up the rocks.

"I'm going to wear you two out if you don't behave," Mr. Kinnebrew said irritably. "It's bad enough we're missing a day's work without having to listen to you two scrapping all the time. Now give a hand unhitching the team."

Coley was a big boy, a year older than Paul, who was eleven. Claude was seven, a year younger than Rose. Rose had seen them at school, but they were in different classrooms for lessons.

Mrs. Kinnebrew, a very proper-looking lady, wore a beautiful lawn dress and her hair pinned up in a tight bun. She carried a dainty white parasol, with ruffles around the edges.

"I don't like to wear a bonnet if I don't have to," she told Mama. "It's too hot in this country."

"You came here from Illinois, didn't you?" Mama asked.

"Yes, and a prosperous little town it was, too," Mrs. Kinnebrew said. "I often wonder what Mr. Kinnebrew could have been thinking when he dragged us all down here. It is a mighty poor excuse for a place to try to dig out a living."

"I wish you would stop making fun of this fine country," Mr. Kinnebrew said. "I never saw a place yet that wouldn't raise a fair crop if farmed right, and I'm going to give this country a good tryout before I give up."

"It is never easy to start over," said Mama. "We are doing it ourselves."

Finally, when the wagons were unloaded, the horses tied up in the shade with buckets of water to drink, and the food assembled for dinner, the children were free to play.

First they threw rocks into the creek to scare away all the cottonmouth snakes so they could swim.

"I hate snakes," Claude said. "There are too many snakes around here."

"You're afraid of everything," Coley scoffed. He was tall and blond. He hurled a skipping stone that skipped almost all the way across the creek. Rose had never seen anything like it. She tried to make stones skip, but they only plopped and sank.

"You're afraid of your own shadow," Coley said with a smirk.

Claude turned red-faced and punched Coley in the side. "I am not either," he shouted. In a second, they were on the ground wrestling.

Rose thought the Kinnebrews were not a very happy family.

Rose waded along the creek bank, hunting crayfish and Indian arrowheads with Paul and George and talking about school. The creek looked so fresh and inviting that Rose wanted to jump right in and get her whole skin wet. But Mama said she must stay dry until after they ate, so she wouldn't have to change twice.

But even if she had been allowed to, Rose did not know how to swim.

When dinner was ready, they all gathered together to eat. The men had dragged logs near the fire to sit on. In the trees around them, cicadas shrilled with raspy sounds that rose and fell, like knives being sharpened on lopsided grindstones.

There were pickles and steaming potatoes that had been roasting in the fire. Mama had brought hard-boiled eggs. Mrs. Cooley had made a big batch of biscuits with snowy white insides, and she passed them around. Everyone admired and enjoyed them.

"How is it, living in town?" Mrs. Kinnebrew asked Mrs. Cooley. "It must certainly be more civilized than living on a farm in the middle of nowhere. I suppose you see many interesting people in the hotel."

"Yes, but we are too busy to visit," said Mrs. Cooley. "It seems all we do is work. And the noise! Just the other day, some farmers tipped over one of the boxcars on the siding."

"Whatever for?" Mr. Kinnebrew asked.

"It was parked right where the tracks cross the road," Mr. Cooley said. "The town asked the railroad to move it three times, but they never did. I guess some fellows took it in their own hands to teach the railroad company a lesson."

"That reminds me of the story about Mr. Arnold's hog," said Mama with a twinkle in her eye. Rose perked right up. She had never heard this story.

"It was in Walnut Grove, Minnesota, one fall at butchering time when a freight train ran over Mr. Arnold's fat hog about halfway up the hill east of town. He couldn't save the meat, but he turned the fat into soap.

"Mr. Arnold tried to get the railroad people to pay him for the hog, as they should have. But they refused.

"So one day, before the freight came through, he went and smeared soap all up and down the track. When the train came along, its wheels spun and spun on the slippery rails. The train crew used up all the sand they were carrying and had to get out and throw dirt on the tracks to get going again.

"Every day after that, the freight train never could get up the grade without sand and trouble. The railroad people were suspicious, but they never could catch Mr. Arnold in the act. Finally the railroad sent a man out to Arnold's one day and paid him cash money for his hog. Sure enough, the very next day the freight went through without any trouble."

Even Mrs. Kinnebrew laughed when Mama finished.

When they had eaten their dinner, they cut and ate the sweating watermelons. The melons were deliciously sweet, and the children competed to see who could spit the seeds farthest.

Finally everyone got changed to go swimming. Mrs. Kinnebrew sat on a log and watched.

Papa swam far out into the deep water. He dove down and disappeared with a splash. Rose held her breath. She waited and waited for Papa to come up again. Rose was just about to scream for Mama when Papa's head popped out of the water, far away downstream from where he had vanished.

Rose wanted to swim with Papa and go under the water. She wanted to see what it was like down there. She walked deeper and deeper into the water until it was up to her chin.

"Don't go in any farther," Mama said.

Suddenly, Papa's dripping wet head rose out of the water, right in front of her. He laughed a great laugh that echoed from the creek bank.

"Will you take me in the deep water, please, Papa?" Rose begged. "I want to disappear under the water."

Papa laughed again. "I think you need a lesson first," he said. "Give me your hands."

Papa took Rose's hands in his own and gently pulled her away from the shallow water. Rose's feet lifted right off the gravel bottom.

"Now I'll hold you up, and you kick your feet," said Papa. Rose kicked as hard as she could. Papa towed her around and around.

She stopped kicking to see if she could touch bottom. But there was nothing there, only deep water. The coldness on her feet scared Rose.

"Keep kicking," said Papa. His smiling face was always in front of her, going backward. "Now I'm going to let go of your hands. You must paddle with your hands, as if you are climbing up a slope, or crawling. And keep kicking, too."

Then Papa let go. Rose paddled as fast and hard as she could. But she could not make her hands and feet go at the same time. She felt herself sinking. Her head went below the surface and she gasped, swallowing a great mouthful of water.

In an instant, she felt Papa's hands lift her up. Rose sputtered and coughed until she could catch her breath.

"I think that is enough for now," Papa said. He towed Rose back to the shallow water.

"Can we do it again, Papa?" Rose begged.

Papa laughed. "I have a better idea," he said. "You can hold on to that old fence rail over there. It will float and you can paddle around. But only so long as I'm watching."

Rose kicked around the creek after that, her arms draped over the fence rail. Sometimes Paul or George would grab on to it, too. They were a ship, sailing on the ocean. The current carried them downstream to a wide shallow place. Then they got out and pushed the fence rail back upstream along the bank and floated down again.

All afternoon they played. There were horseshoes to throw. They cut cane and fished for a while, but no one caught any fish.

Finally all the play was drained out of Rose. She lay on her back on a wide, flat stone that was big enough for her whole body. She looked into the sky at piles of fat, white clouds floating above the trees. She turned over on her stomach, stretched her arms out to the side, and felt the warmth of the rock soaking into her body.

She loved that summery day. It seemed to Rose that summer could soothe every care and heal every hurt.

SPELLDOWN

They went picnicking two more times that summer. By the last time, Rose had learned how to swim in deep water. But she never did unless Papa was with her. Deep water still frightened her.

At school, Rose stayed at the head of the line in spelling, although often it was very close. Blanche was a good speller and she only missed the hardest words. Some days when Rose sat reading her book at dinner, she noticed Blanche studying her reader.

One morning, Professor Kay stood before the class with a grave look on his face.

"I have an announcement to make which is very sad," he said. "Irene Strong, who has been out of school these many weeks with diphtheria, has crossed to that other shore from which no traveler returns."

Rose was confused. She leaned across the aisle toward the boy sitting in the next row. "What did he say?" she whispered.

"She's gone and died," the boy hissed. "Irene's died."

"We will bow our heads now for a minute of silent prayer," said Professor Kay.

Rose was too stunned to think of praying. The only person she had ever known who had died was her little brother. But she had been only a baby then herself. She didn't really remember anything at all.

Irene had not been Rose's friend, but she had sat right next to Rose. Then she had a new thought. What if she caught diphtheria? Would she die? And what would become of Mama and Papa if Rose died? They would never have other children. Mama had said so. Who would help on the farm?

The thought of Mama and Papa alone was the most unbearable of all. She fought back a sob. She could hear some of the other children muttering their prayers. Someone was sniffling.

Professor Kay did not need to raise his voice or punish anyone all the rest of that week. Rose wished she could move her seat, but all the other seats were full. She could not help thinking of poor Irene whenever she looked at the empty spot beside her.

The days flew by and summer grew old and dusty. Soon they would have their first harvest from the new farm.

September came, and the last day of the summer school session drew near. Professor Kay announced on Monday that there would be a special spelldown on Friday after supper. Then there would be no more school until after harvest time, in December.

"Each classroom will have its own spelldown," Professor Kay explained. "Your mothers and fathers are invited to come and attend. There will be refreshments after and a prize for the winner."

Rose was terribly excited and jittery all that

week. She knew she could win the spelldown. She had gotten almost all the headmarks in the class. But Blanche was getting better and better. She had gotten three headmarks when Rose made mistakes.

On Friday afternoon, the students scrubbed the whole classroom until it shone. Professor Kay stood on a chair and tacked paper chains the students had made around the windows. When the classroom was spotless and decorated, school was dismissed.

Rose dashed home to do her chores and get ready. Mama had washed and ironed Rose's best calico. After supper, they all washed up, got dressed, and walked to school together.

When they got to the top of Patterson's Hill, Rose and Mama slipped on the stockings and shoes they had been carrying as the sun began to melt into a puddle of gold. Rose swallowed hard as they walked down the hill into the schoolyard.

At the door of Rose's classroom, Professor Kay greeted Mama and Papa and invited them inside.

"Good to see you folks again," he said. "Come on in and have a seat."

School looked very different with all the grown-ups milling about. Rose spied Blanche, standing with her parents. Blanche's red serge dress was even more beautiful than the dresses she wore every day.

Finally Professor Kay asked all of the students to take their places against the wall and for all of the parents to be seated.

"We are honored to have all the parents here this evening," he said as the scuffling and murmuring faded away.

Then Professor Kay led the audience in singing a song. After that, there were recitations by two other students. Finally the spelldown began.

Rose was very nervous as the two warm-up rounds started, but she soon relaxed. Anyone could spell these words: *kettle, beyond, mouse.* Rose looked at Mama and Papa and smiled.

Then the real spelldown began and the words got harder, and trickier.

"Counsel," pronounced Stanley Walters, the boy standing ahead of Rose. "C-o-u-n, *coun,* s-i-l, *sil. Counsel.*"

"I'm sorry. That is wrong," Professor Kay said. Stanley shrugged and hung his head as he shuffled out of line to go sit with his mother and father. Rose liked starting out at the foot of the line. It gave her heart to hear other students making mistakes.

"Next."

"*Counsel,*" Rose said confidently. "C-o-u-n, *coun,* s-e-l, *sel. Counsel.*"

One by one, the students were spelled down and left the line to join their families.

"*Constructed,*" Blanche said slowly, as if she were confused. "C-o-n, *con,* s-t-r-u . . ." She hesitated. Rose's heart fluttered. "C, *struc,* t-e-d, *ted. Constructed,*" Blanche said, with a little sigh.

"That's my girl," Blanche's father whispered loudly. Blanche blushed and stared down at her shoes.

Soon there were only three students standing: Rose, Blanche, and a redheaded boy named Oscar Hensley.

"*Sheaves,*" Professor Kay said.

"*Sheaves,*" Oscar repeated. "S-h-e-e-v-e-s, *sheaves.*"

"I'm sorry, Oscar. That is wrong." Professor Kay said.

Now Rose felt every eye in the room on her. She and Blanche were the only students left. Blanche got the first word. Then Rose, then Blanche. On and on they spelled, into the evening. Rose's mouth had grown dry, and she desperately wanted to sit down.

"*Occasion,*" Professor Kay said.

"*Occasion,*" Rose repeated. Her mind went blank. "*Occasion,*" she said again. Her thoughts raced. One "c" or two; one "s" or two? Her chest tightened and she felt herself gasping for breath.

She looked at Mama and Papa. Papa was twirling his mustache. Mama twisted her handkerchief in her hands.

"*Occasion,*" Rose said a third time. All the shuffling and fidgeting in the room came to a stop. Everyone was staring at Rose.

Rose was too terrified to speak. She didn't known which it was, two "c"s or two "s"s! Or two "c"s *and* two "s"s. Which was it?

"Do you wish me to repeat the word and define it?" Professor Kay said gently.

"No," Rose croaked. She must try, even if she got it wrong. She closed her eyes tight, trying to see that word in her mind.

"Occasion," she said slowly. "O-c, *oc* . . . c-a, *ca,* s-i-o-n, *sion. Occasion."*

"Good girl!" Papa called out rather loudly. Nervous laughter broke out in the room. Mama's hand flew to her mouth.

"Correct," Professor Kay said. Rose let out a shivery sigh.

There were four more rounds of perfect spelling. Then Professor Kay gave Blanche the word *precipice.*

"Precipice," Blanche said slowly.

"P-r-e, *pre,* c-i, *ci,* p-i . . . s-e, *pice. Precipice."*

"Oh!" someone in the audience cried out. Papa slapped his hand on the desktop. Mama turned and shushed him.

Professor Kay said, "Wrong."

Rose could hardly believe her ears. She knew how to spell that word.

Professor Kay looked at Rose. *"Precipice,"* he said.

"Precipice," said Rose. "P-r-e, *pre,* c-i, *ci,*

p-i . . . c-e, *pice. Precipice.*"

The room erupted in a swirl of shouting and clapping and confusion. Suddenly everyone was on his feet, moving about and talking. Mama and Papa came pushing through the crowd up to Rose. Papa gave her a big hug, and Mama smiled her biggest smile.

Rose realized with a shock that she had actually won the spelldown.

"That's our smart girl," Papa said. "You did it! You beat 'em all hollow."

"We are very proud of you," said Mama.

Then Professor Kay was there. "Very well done, young lady," he said. "Here is your prize, well deserved, I must say, close as it was."

He handed Rose a book. It was heavy and thickly covered with soft red plush. Inscribed on the cover in shiny gold lettering was the word *Autographs.*

Mama said it was an album, for friends and loved ones to write little sayings and poems in. It was a place to keep memories of good friends and special times.

"Every girl must have one," said Mama. "I did."

Rose looked at all the beautiful blank pages. She trembled with excitement to think of those empty pages filling up with words no one had thought of yet.

Rose was jumping with joy inside her skin, but she said politely, "Thank you, Professor Kay."

But when Rose spotted Blanche across the room, her joy began to melt into something else. Blanche stood slump-shouldered with her face buried in her mother's bosom. Her father was patting her on the head and saying something to her. Rose thought about how close she herself had come to losing.

Rose looked at her beautiful new album, and then back at Blanche. Blanche had been unkind to Rose, yet Rose did not hate her.

But Rose did hate to be the cause of Blanche's tears. She thought about what she could do. Then, in a flash, something came to her.

Rose walked across the schoolroom, right up to Blanche's family.

"Why, hello there, young lady," said Mr. Coday. "You really gave us quite a show here tonight."

Blanche's cheeks were damp and her face was blotched. Her reddened eyes flashed at Rose and her mouth pinched itself into a frown.

"Please don't cry," said Rose. "I'm sorry you lost. I almost lost first. I couldn't remember if *occasion* has one 'c' or two. I only guessed. I was just lucky."

Blanche's frown softened. She looked down at the autograph album in Rose's hands.

"Professor Kay gave me this for winning. It isn't fair to give only one prize when we are such equally good spellers," said Rose. "We can share it, if you like."

Rose held out the album.

Blanche stared at it with disbelieving eyes.

"Well, isn't that something?" Mrs. Coday said. Then she nudged Blanche with her elbow. "Have you lost your tongue?" she said sharply.

"Thank you," Blanche murmured.

"That's a fine gesture, young lady," Mr. Coday said quickly. "You are an example to us all. But a memory album, now, that isn't a thing easily shared. Besides, you did win it, fair and square, luck or no."

"Yes," Blanche said, the storm clearing from her face. "It is your prize. You must keep it for yourself. But thank you. You are very nice to offer."

Rose thought for a moment. Then she had another idea.

"Will you write in it, then?" Rose asked. "Since we are both the best spellers, I would like you to be the first one to write in it."

"I . . . I wouldn't know what to write," Blanche stammered. Then she blushed.

"Take it home with you," said Rose. "Then you can think of something."

Mr. Coday said that, since the school session was over, he could give it to Papa when he came into the drugstore.

"All right," said Blanche softly. She took the album from Rose and carefully tucked it under her arm. Now she looked at Rose with shining eyes and smiled. "I'll take good care of it. I promise."

"Good-bye, Blanche," Rose said.

"Good-bye, Rose," said Blanche.

Rose skipped back to be with Mama and Papa, who were still talking to Professor Kay. People were leaving the room and going upstairs for lemonade. Rose tugged Mama's skirt and whispered in her ear, *"Lemonade."*

Mama laughed. "Very well," she said. "But where is your album?"

"I gave it to Blanche. She is going to write something in it."

"That's very sweet, Rose," said Mama. "Now I have two reasons to be proud of you tonight. A good winner is a gracious winner."

Blanche did not come upstairs to drink lemonade. Rose did not see her again the rest of the evening. But as she walked home in the dark between Mama and Papa, Rose remembered Blanche's grateful smile. It made Rose happy to think she could make someone smile.

Harvest Moon

School was over until December, and summer was drawing to a close. There was no time for play now, for this was the month of the harvest moon. They must hurry to gather in the crops before frost.

Harvesting potatoes was a treasure hunt. Papa walked along the rows with the shovel and loosened up the hardened hills of earth. Then Rose dug with her hands into the loose soil until she found the pale yellow potatoes clinging to the roots. She made sure to get every one, even the tiniest buttons.

They stacked the potatoes in piles between

the rows. Mama separated the good ones out to sell. When they were done, she and Rose put the graded potatoes into sacks. Then Papa loaded the heavy sacks onto the wagon and drove into town. Rose swelled with pride to see the food she had helped grow going off to market.

That night after supper Papa went to the mantel and got down a little book he often wrote in. He sat by the fireplace and scribbled some numbers in pencil. Papa called it his accounts book. He wrote down everything they bought, traded, and sold.

"Why?" asked Rose.

"Any farmer worth his salt keeps his records," said Papa. "It tells how we're doing. See here," he said, showing her the book. Its pages were filled with writing and numbers.

"Every time we trade at Reynolds's, I write that down in one column," Papa explained. "That's a minus. Every time I sell a load of wood, or potatoes, or Mama sends in eggs, I write it down in another column. That is a plus.

"When it comes settling-up time, after the harvest is all in, I will add all the minuses and all the pluses and I can see which one is greater."

"What does it say now?" Rose asked. "Are we plus or minus?"

Papa laughed. "Too soon to say for sure, Rose. But we're getting by."

Papa's account book was a little confusing, but Rose understood that it was very important.

The next day, they dug up the sweet potatoes and set the gnarled roots out on planks to dry in the sunshine. When the sweet potatoes were dry, Rose and Mama wrapped each one in a scrap of old newspaper. Then they put all the wrapped potatoes in a wooden box in a corner of the kitchen.

They gathered chestnuts that had fallen from a tree near the orchard. Mama packed them in layers of salt in a big pickling jar. She tucked the jar away in one of the trunks where they wouldn't be tempted to eat them. She was saving them for Christmas.

One night at supper, after Papa had been to town, he laid Rose's autograph album on the table. Rose opened it at once and looked on the first page. Blanche had written something there in blue ink. Mama peered over Rose's shoulder and read:

Too wise you are, too wise you be;
I see you are too wise for me.
Your friend, Blanche Coday. October 3, 1895.

Rose tingled with excitement when she read the words "Your friend."

"That's very sweet," said Mama. "I suspect your book will fill up quickly when you go back to school in December."

"I want you and Papa to write something, too," Rose said.

When the dishes had been cleared, Papa took Mama's pen, twisted his mustache for a few minutes, and then scratched away at the page. Rose fidgeted impatiently. Then Papa carefully blotted the page with Mama's blotter and showed it to Rose.

To my prairie Rose:
Be faithful in all things,
Superficial in none,

And always remember,
that home is home.
—Papa.

Mama said she must think about what to write. The next Sunday, she spent a long time writing in Rose's book. When she was done, she showed Rose what she had written.

There were some naughty flowers once,
Who were careless in their play;
They got their petals torn and soiled
As they swung in the dust all day.

They went to bed at four o'clock,
With faces covered tight,
To keep the fairy, Drop O'Dew,
From washing them at night.

Poor Drop O'Dew! What could she do?
She said to the Fairy Queen,
"I cannot get those Four O'clocks
To keep their faces clean."

The mighty Storm King heard the tale;
"My winds and rain," roared he,
"Shall wash those naughty flowers well,
As flowers ought to be."

So raindrops came and caught them all
Before they went to bed,
And washed those little Four O'clocks
At three o'clock instead.

Mama's poem was beautiful, as good as any in Rose's *McGuffey's Reader*. Rose read it over and over again, and liked it better each time.

One morning before the first rooster crow, Rose woke up with a start. A sound had disturbed her sleep, but she didn't know what it was. Mama and Papa were still asleep. The wind was still and the woods quiet. A square of bright moonlight from the window lay on the floor at the foot of her bed. It was so bright inside that Rose could read the clock face. It was three o'clock.

Then Rose heard the sound again. It was a wild howling, far away. Then more howling and baying, in different voices. Rose had never heard wolves crying before, but she thought for sure that was what it must be.

She crept out of bed and tiptoed across the cold floor into the kitchen. Fido got up from his sleeping place by the stove and stretched with a tiny moan. Then he tapped across the floor and stood at Rose's feet.

Rose went to the front door and opened it. It complained with a tiny squeak. She stepped out onto the porch and looked up at the moon through an opening in the trees. The bright circle of light was clothed in a fuzzy halo that was brownish around the edge.

It was a harvest moon, when the moon is so bright farmers can work into the night gathering the crops. It was too bright to see the man in the moon's face. Rose had to look away.

She sat on the porch and stared hard all around her. The shadows seemed as crisp as daylight, but the harder she looked, the more they were smoothed and softened, the way moss softens a rock. Her eyes kept playing tricks on her.

The gathering mist made the air glow in places. She could see the dark outlines of spiders asleep in their webs in the eaves of the porch, waiting for the earth to warm up and send them a morning meal. Rose felt herself part of the night.

A creaking floorboard in the kitchen startled her. Mama appeared in the doorway, ghostly white in her nightgown.

"Is something the matter?" she asked.

"Something was howling in the woods," said Rose. "I thought it was wolves."

"I heard it, too," said Mama, sitting next to Rose on the porch's edge. She yawned. "But it isn't wolves. I think it is just some farmer out hunting a raccoon with his hounds."

They sat in silence for a moment. Rose shivered against the cool morning air. Mama put her arm around Rose's shoulder and squeezed. Then the ghostly shape of Blackfoot came padding toward them across the yard from the barn where he had been sleeping. He mewed softly and rubbed against their legs, purring loudly in the stillness.

"The moonlight is lovely, isn't it?" said Mama. "It's as though you were inside a dream. You can see everything, but you can't see it, either."

Rose sat cuddled up against Mama for the longest time, watching the mist floating quietly into the moon-washed yard. She wished that moment could go on forever.

But just then the rooster crowed. A new day was about to begin.

Read more about Rose's adventures in

IN THE **LAND** OF THE
BIG RED APPLE
by **ROGER LEA MacBRIDE**

Are We Poor?

Papa drove the rattling wagon slowly along the twisting road through the steep Ozark hills, so slowly that Rose wanted to jump off the wagon seat and run ahead. She silently tried to hurry along the mares, Pet and May. They would never get to Mr. Rippee's at this pace!

Finally the team turned off the road into a wagon track that climbed a hillside. The horses bent their necks and grunted as they pulled the wagon into a great field that soared up in front of them. In that field were lines and lines of apple trees, more than anyone could possibly count. The trees marched across the sloping hillside like an army of bushy-headed soldiers. Everywhere Rose looked, she could see people picking fruit and filling baskets.

This was their future, Rose thought as Papa *whoa*ed the mares and pushed up his hat brim to see better. He uttered a satisfied, "Mmm-mmm."

Mama sighed. "I don't think there's any crop as lovely as apples."

"In a couple years, our place'll look as fine as this," Papa said. "Then, my prairie Rose, we'll be rich." He gave Rose a wink and smiled at Mama.

"Rich." Rose repeated the word in her thoughts. She couldn't imagine the spindly little apple trees in their own orchard ever growing big enough to be heavy with fruit. And she certainly couldn't imagine being rich.

Rose wore the same dress every day, for a whole school session. Only when it became tattered or too small could Rose go with Mama to Reynolds's Store and pick out cloth for a new one. No matter how scuffed and patched her shoes might become, they also had to last.

And her set of hair ribbons, one for each of her braids, were meant to last as long as her dress, although Rose sometimes lost them playing.

Some of the town girls teased Rose, calling her "country girl."

But she knew she wasn't really a country girl, at least not like the poor girls who came to school with dirty feet and runny noses. It made Rose's neck burn with shame to be called a country girl.

Rose looked at Mr. Rippee's fine orchard and asked Mama and Papa, "Are we poor?"

Mama drew her shawl around her shoulders. "I think you had better answer that, Manly. You're the one who put the thought in her head."

"Now, I wouldn't say we're poor, exactly," Papa said thoughtfully, twisting an end of his mustache. "We've got our own spread. Folks who have land have their freedom, which is a sight better than money any day."

"We aren't poor, Rose," Mama said. "But the going is rough right now. Things will get better again. It takes time.

"Besides," she added, "as your grandpa Ingalls always says, the rich man gets his ice in the summer, and the poor man gets it in the winter. It all evens up in the end."

Now Mama and Papa looked at Mr. Rippee's orchard with searching, hopeful eyes.

Rose knew that in their future, whole families would travel from all around the countryside to pick apples from their orchard. When that day came, she and Mama and Papa would have everything they ever wanted.

It had been a bit more than a year since they first came to the little town of Mansfield, Missouri, from the burned-out prairie in Dakota. They called their forty-acre place Rocky Ridge Farm, because it sat on a rocky ridge. How everything had changed in just that year! Rose was nearly nine years old now, old enough to do most any chore on the farm.

The fall before, they had started out with a drafty log house and a few sacks of food. Now they had their own field of corn, and a harvest of potatoes, and onions, and cabbage, a small crop of oats, and a whole summer of wonderful eating from the garden. Best of all, they had the tender young apple saplings, nearly a thousand in all, that were left behind by the man who had sold them the farm. All they had to do was tend them a little and wait for their first harvest.

Papa was right, Rose decided. They weren't poor. But still, four years until the first apple crop seemed an eternity. Trees grew so slowly!

LITTLE HOUSE

LITTLE HOUSE · BIG ADVENTURE

LITTLE HOUSE IN THE BIG WOODS

FARMER BOY

LITTLE HOUSE ON THE PRAIRIE

ON THE BANKS OF PLUM CREEK

BY THE SHORES OF SILVER LAKE

THE LONG WINTER

LITTLE TOWN ON THE PRAIRIE

THESE HAPPY GOLDEN YEARS

THE FIRST FOUR YEARS

THE MARTHA YEARS

LITTLE HOUSE IN THE HIGHLANDS
MELISSA WILEY

THE FAR SIDE OF THE LOCH
MELISSA WILEY

THE CHARLOTTE YEARS

LITTLE HOUSE BY BOSTON BAY
MELISSA WILEY

ON TIDE MILL LANE
MELISSA WILEY

THE CAROLINE YEARS

LITTLE HOUSE IN BROOKFIELD
MARIA D. WILKES

LITTLE TOWN AT THE CROSSROADS
MARIA D. WILKES

THE ROSE YEARS

LITTLE HOUSE ON ROCKY RIDGE
ROGER LEA MacBRIDE

LITTLE FARM IN THE OZARKS
ROGER LEA MacBRIDE